Howard Llewellyn Swisher

## Briar Blossoms

Being a Collection of a Few Verses and Some Prose

Howard Llewellyn Swisher

**Briar Blossoms**
*Being a Collection of a Few Verses and Some Prose*

ISBN/EAN: 9783337416522

Printed in Europe, USA, Canada, Australia, Japan

Cover: Foto ©Andreas Hilbeck / pixelio.de

More available books at **www.hansebooks.com**

# Briar ✦ ✦
# Blossoms,

Being a Collection of a Few
Verses and Some Prose . . .

BY ··

HOWARD LLEWELLYN SWISHER.

1899.
ACME PUBLISHING COMPANY,
MORGANTOWN, W. VA.

To

# Mr. John Wallace,

OF

WHEELING.

A good Fellow and a Writer of

Clever Verses.

# Preface,

E'en a Good Story too often Told
Provokes a Smile because it's old,

# Things You Read About.

|  | PAGE |
|---|---|
| Some Glimpses of Yosemite | 9 |
| The Sleigh Bells | 15 |
| A Lonely Grave | 16 |
| Bohemian Love Song | 17 |
| Despair | 18 |
| Black Man or White | 19 |
| A Little Flirt | 24 |
| Minnehaha | 25 |
| Mammy's Boy | 27 |
| Lottie Doon | 30 |
| The Spring Neath the Old Gum Tree | 32 |
| A Song of the Northland | 33 |
| My Rival | 34 |
| In West Virginia | 37 |
| Recollections of an Old Bachelor | 38 |
| Shooting Stars | 40 |
| The Revelation of Harry Sheldon | 42 |
| Noel | 45 |
| Books | 46 |
| A Rondolet | 47 |
| The Mysterious Brooch | 48 |
| Le Feever's Confession | 52 |
| A Song of Today | 56 |
| Selections from Abdiolel | 57 |
| The Lost Child | 68 |
| Them Frogs | 70 |
| Spring Equinox | 71 |

Good Night..
A Recollection
Alumni Poem...
The Island of Despair.
Reciprocity............
The Poet..............................
Requital...................
A Translation ..............................
Medley..........................
Success—M. S. Cornwell ....................
When Dad Strikes I'le—John Wallace ... ....
The Marriners Love  Geo. M. Ford............
The Dead Sure Thing—J. M. Kunkle........
On Tumble Down Street- C. Luke Michael.
Yesterday—Jas. W. Horn......................
Isle of Going-to-be—C. Luke Michael..........
The Little White Kerchief— C. Luke Michael
I'm Goin' Home fer Christmas —John Wallace..
Expectation - J. Cal. Watkins.................
A Sylvan Tragedy—Alice Piersol Cain..... ....

# Briar Blossoms.

# Some Glimpses of Yosemite.

"The vulgar know not all the hidden pockets,
Where Nature stows away her lovliness."

He who has failed to see Yosemite Valley has missed one of life's choice pleasures. Nestled in the heart of the Sierras, lies this scenic wonder, this gigantic assemblage of peaks and canons, overshadowed by the Himalayas alone and not surpassed for ruggedness even by the Andes themselves.

No railroad leads directly to it; in fact not nearer than fifty miles. At Barenda the main line of the Southern Pacific is left and a branch line carries you to Raymond, a small station among the foothills.

Two days by stage are necessary to complete the journey to Yosemite. More than 10,000 feet of ascent is necessary to reach the highest peak of the Valley from Raymond.

The first day we will ascend 8000 feet, only to descend 4000 feet to Wawona to spend the night. This day's drive will not be without its pleasures, especially if the time is spring. Green hills rise all around, crested with a few rude digger pines, white oaks of stunted growth with knotted arms overshadow the way, while here and there a live oak spreads its intricate branches, with their shining green leaves forming a a hiding place for the shy blue quails that peep at us as we pass.

Night finds us at Wawona, where is situated a fine hotel for the accommodation of tourists, and a place in itself not lacking attractions, but we are tending to Yosemite and will pass it by unnoticed.

Twenty-five miles yet intervene between us and the Mecca of our pilgrimage. Wawona is at an elevation of 4000 feet, equal to that of the floor of the Valley, but the stage road leads over a mountain 6000 or 7000 feet in height; hence some climbing is necessary during the second day's travel. The scenery is changed from what we saw yesterday. The scrubby oaks have given way to lofty yellow and sugar pines which, together with the graceful redwood, cast sombre shadows over the roadway.

The flowers too have changed. We no longer see the fuzzy lupines, the nodding calochortus or the flaming California poppy. Instead, an occasional snow plant raises its accusing countenance dripping blood red, a mountain flag, or the showy flowers of the leatherwood tree are our companions. On we go over a gentle rise or down a steep declivity. There the road hugs close to the mountain wall and we gaze into the depths below, now we travel along the top of a forested ridge.

But we are nearing the end of our journey. Around a sudden turn we dash and the driver draws his reins. We have reached Inspiration Point. This place is not misnamed. It is here the first full view of Yosemite Valley greets the eye of the weary tourist, who has traveled perhaps thousands of miles for no other purpose than to behold its wonders. Two thousand feet below lies the verdant valley sleeping in its mountain fastness. Looking eastward one can take in the entire valley. About seven miles in length; in width from one-half to one mile.

Through it glides the placid Merced, giving little token of the mighty leaps it has made to reach this channel, and less indication of its yet rugged ramblings. Beside it a chance wigwam of the Yosemite or Grizzly Bear Indians is seen, but they have continually dwindled away since the discovery of the valley by white men in 1851. On either side of the valley rise granite walls, varying in height from 2000 to 3000 feet. Here moulded into a solid faced wall, there shooting into peaks, some smooth, others jagged and rough. Over these walls pour various streams, some mere threads, some creeks and rivers, forming the most wonderful cataracts in the world.

After we had looked until weary, the driver snapped his whip and soon we were winding down the side of the mountain into the valley. It was in May, 1894, that we visited this valley, although we arrived earlier in the season than the full tide of visitors sets in, I think we could scarcely have chosen a more propitious time, for as it happened we got to see the valley in both its winter and spring loveliness. It had been summer weather for more than a month in the San Joaquin valley, and the snow, even in this high altitude, was almost gone, except on the higher peaks, where it lays all summer. A rain began about midnight, and in the morning what a change! Has winter returned in all its iciness? So it would seem, for what was at night covered with flowers and grass is now carpeted with snow. A great transfiguration certainly, but not lacking in the beauty.

The old peaks looked very venerable with their hoary crowns. The trees that fringed the edges of the cliffs were not burdened by snow, but seemed crystalized. Every branch, twig, and leaf had a glossy coat, which made the rays of the full faced sun, that now looked wonderingly on the scene, dance and twinkled for joy.

The valley lies almost due east and west, with an arm branching to the southeast and, as we have noticed, is hemmed in by high walls which here and there rise into lofty peaks. On the northern side of the valley, at the western end, stands El Captain, a huge, solid faced cliff rising vertically 3300 feet above the valley floor, thus making its summit over seven thousand feet above sea level. In saying that the cliff's face is vertical we make a slight mistake; it really leans out one hundred feet or more toward the valley, giving one the unpleasant sensation as he stands at its base and looks upward at it, that he is about to be crushed.

On the same side of the valley are the Three Brothers, so

called because three sons of Teneya, the last chief of the Yosemite Indians, were captured at this spot by the white men in
1851. The highest of these, Eagle Peak, is near 4000 feet.
Further up we pass Yosemite Point and Washington Tower.
At the eastern end of the valley we find ourselves between two
immense granite masses, known as North Dome and South
Dome. The former rising 3700 feet above the smooth surface
of Mirror Lake, which lies between them.

Closing the aperture at this end of the valley is Cloud Rest,
nearly 6000 feet high. Back of South Dome are Grizzly Peak
and Liberty Cap, both towering shafts of stone. Still farther
down on the southern side of the valley is Glacier Point. On
the same side, opposite Yosemite Point, is Sentinel Rock, on
whose almost inaccessible summit floated a flag placed there by
the hand of a lady adventurer. Below this and facing El Captain
stand Cathedral Rocks, adjoining Cathedral Spires. These
spires rise from the rocky height of two thousand feet, shooting their slender columns 700 feet further into space.

The waterfalls form no secondary attraction. They, like the
peaks, cliffs, and domes are many and beautiful; but we pause
for only three or four: The first one seen on entering the valley
is the Bridal Veil Fall. Here the waters of Phono Creek pour
over the southern wall 600 feet into the Merced. This fall is
well named. The wind gently waves the spray to and fro as
a breath might move the real bridal veil, and in the evening
when the sun causes a rainbow to play in its midst, one can
easily imagine he sees behind the veil the glowing cheeks of a
blushing bride.

Through the southern arm of the valley enters Merced
River. On this we find both the Vernal and the Nevada Falls.
The Nevada is farthest up the river and is the highest. Over
it the Merced, a stream about 100 feet wide, dashes itself on
the rocks 650 below. It looks not unlike a huge avalanche of
snow as it churns its waters into whiteness and foam. About
a mile below this is Vernal Falls, not so high but more beau-

tiful. These falls are only 350 feet high, small as compared with the others, but more than twice as high as Niagara. Advancing near the foot of the falls, though the spray rains heavily, one sees a peculiar spectacle. Each of the falls at the proper time of day has its beautiful rainbows. But here was something different. A circle of rainbow colors, whose edge just reached my feet, quivered in a horizontal plane. I stood gazing in wonder upon this pleasing phenomenon until I was thoroughly drenched by the spray. I then moved nearer the base of the fall, but the circle still tremblingly followed. After watching it about an hour, the sun having changed its position, the glowing colors melted into the silver spray.

It would be unpardonable to attempt a sketch of Yosemite without noting its greatest attraction, Yosemite Falls. That wonderful cataract which is higher than the three waterfalls of Southland combined; eights times more lofty than the Victoria Falls, and equaling in height sixteen Niagaras. Here the waters of Yosemite Creek, fresh from the snowy fountains, cast themselves down 2634 feet. There are three divisions of the Falls: first, a vertical plunge of sixteen hundred feet; second, a series of cascades, where in a distance of one-eighth mile a descent of over 400 feet is made, and then a final leap of 600 feet.

I climbed to the top of the Falls, May 15, 1894, through the snow and wet, and though tired from the journey I was fully repaid. At the top of the Falls is a railing firmly imbedded in the granite. Over this one can lean and see the water rush past him one instant and the next see it seething and boiling in its rocky cauldron 1600 feet below. As I watched it the prismatic colors were playing hide and seek among the spray dashed off in the descent. It was reluctantly that I left the place.

Let us not leave this wonderland until we have taken a peep into its looking glass—Mirror Lake. This lake lies at the eastern end of the valley. It is only a few hundred yards in circumference, is walled in by some of the highest peaks and domes of the valley and supplied with water by Teneya Creek. To enjoy its peculiar reflective power one must be at the lake before sunrise. Then one sees reflected, with all the faithfulness of the most polished mirror, all the objects which surround the lake, from the impending cliffs and vast domes to the trembling bush that clings to its sides. Most beautiful of all is the reflected sunrise. To watch it is to realize the inability of Art to rival the beauties of Nature. Sitting at the water's edge and looking steadily at the reflected summit of the opposite dome, one sees the approach of sun, heralded by the brightening of a portion of the sky. If there be light clouds floating by they will be mellowed into a bright golden color as they pass. Soon one sees the sun like a burnished star peep shyly over the mountain top; in a moment more a line of liquid silver runs along the crest of the granite mass, a beautiful gilding; soon a burning crescent appears and in a few minutes the sun, full faced, is swaying to and fro in the rippling lake.

Eight days have too quickly passed since our arrival in Yosemite. As we stand again on Inspiration Point for a farewell view, a feeling well described in the lines of L. H. Bunnell, Yosemite's discoverer, comes to us:

> "But now farewell, Yosemite:
> If thou appears not again in sight,
>   Thou'lt come, I know, in life's extremity
> While passing into realms of light"

# The Sleigh Bells.

Hear the far off tiny tinkle
Of the sleigh bells as they sprinkle,
Their faint tintinabulations on the crisp
    and frosty air.
While the snow so white and airy
Like the death shroud of a fairy,
Spreads a sparkling diamond carpet 'round about
    us everywhere.

Hear the hoof-beats sounding nearer,
And the laughter ringing clearer,
As the steaming steeds sweep past us like the
    winter's windy blast.
See the lovers faces beaming,
And their fur robes backward streaming
Like the long hair of Mazeppa mounting up
    the mountain pass.

Sweet the youthful silver laughter,
Sharp the house dog's barking after,
Beats the erstwhile silent night air into throbbing
    waves of sound.
Soft the silent mellow moonlight,
Bright the sparkling crystal starlight,
Harsh the horses horny hoofbeats falling on
    the frozen ground.

They have passed the happy people
While the church bell in the steeple
Strikes the silent hour of midnight to the country
    all around.
Softly now the sleighbells whisper,
Soft as angels song at vesper,
Then the great deep gulf of silence swallows up
    the waves of sound.

## A Lonely Grave.

Wandering lonely in the forest shade,
  Far from dwelling and man's abode,
I chanced upon a lonely grave,
  As carefully I sought my devious road.

No slab of marble marked the place,
  To tell of good deeds that were done;
By him who slept, had closed his race,
  And kept his rest beneath the mossed headstone,

The only watchers were the sturdy oaks,
  The only mourners were the sighing pines,
As round their forms they drew their cloaks,
  More beautiful than silk, or soft ermine.

Across the mound the shadows fell
  As if to shade it from a profane eye.
Who slept beneath I could not tell,
  Nor was the secret meant for such as I.

Perchance some mother's only son,
  The staff and comfort of her age;
Leaving his home his race to run,
  Without the narrow limits of his cage.

Yet if not this, perhaps a brother,
  Meeting his death in this sad place,
Was mourned by sister, most a mother,
  When she no longer could his footsteps trace.

Or then if not, mayhap some lover,
  Searching for fortune and for fame,
That he might give it to another,
  To whose long willing arms he never came.

But whence he came or how he died,
  There's to tell me none to say.
I'll leave him sleeping on the mountain side,
  And wander weary on my winding way.

Burrough, Cal., April 1, 1894.

## Bohemian Love Song.

We're poor, dear heart, but we will feign
That we a castle have in Spain.
When clouds are dark and storms rage high,
Together we will thither fly.
Around it spreads the living green,
Above it bends the smiling sky.
'Twas meant, dear love, that you and I
Should reign within as king and queen.

We're sad, dear heart, but we will feign
That we a castle have in Spain,
Where tears flow not and hearts are light;
Where lips are red and eyes are bright.
The castle walls a splendor fling
Upon the beauty-dazzled eye.
'Tis meant, my love, that you and I
Should there be reigning queen and king.

We're faint, dear heart, but we will feign
That we a castle have in Spain.
There love doth yield a magic spell
And faith and hope together dwell.
The windows dance a diamond sheen,
The slim spires sparkle toward the sky.
I'm sure, my love, that you and I
Shall ere long reign there king and queen.

Though we are poor and sad and faint,
And most o'ercome by sad distraint,
Mid all, my love, we'll ever feign
That we a castle have in Spain.

## Despair.

I said :  "I'll all my passions satisfy,
  And smothering, drown them in a satiate sea."
This I find, the more I gratify
  They greater grow, and choking, consume me.

# Black Man or White.

Robert Burton was a waiter in a hotel in a southern city where I had gone to spend the winter. Almost the first day of my stay at the hotel I was struck with Robert's independent and intelligent face. His companion waiters were all negroes of various degrees of blackness, but so white was Robert that I was puzzled to know whether or not his color was the climatic tan or due to negro blood. His bearing and conversation, as I became better acquainted with him at daily meals, left me in still deeper doubt. For a person in his position and of his race (if indeed he was a negro) he seemed so gentlemanly, so intelligent, so much above his surroundings, that, I at last, to satisfy myself, asked him whether or not he was a negro. Evidently surprised at my question he answered calmly in the affirmative.

"How does it happen, Robert," I then asked him, "that you have acquired an education?"

"My mother" said he, "taught me a great many things in books and afterwards master gave me money to attend a school in Ohio for two years."

"But how does it come you are now a hotel waiter when you are fitted for something better?"

He flushed at this, but replied firmly: "My benefactor is dead. Others do not take so much interest in me as he did and I have to make a living for myself and mother."

"But surely," I went on, "you need not do such work as this. Why do you not do something more respectable and something in which you could turn your education to account."

"What is there I can do?" said he. "In this southern country negroes are only fit for servitude, and from what I have learned from those who live in the North they are little better off there. Do you know," he continued, and with a touch of irony in his voice, "of any negroes in your state who hold positions of trust, who are in mercantile business for themselves, who are clerks or shopkeepers in white communities?"

I answered that I did not, and as the conversation was growing disagreeable it was dropped.

That night I thought much of what Robert Burton had said. I had taken a strong liking to him. 'Negroes are only fit for servitude,' again and again this saying came to my mind. Alas, it was too true. Visiting the curses of the fathers upon the children, not only unto the third and fourth generation, but through countless ages. It did not seem just, yet it was natural and true. He was a man with only a tinge of slave blood in his veins, but for that he was condemned to serve.

At last I thought of a plan whereby at least this one might escape the curse that rested on his fathers.

"Robert," I said the next evening, "come to my room to-night, when your work is done. I have something to say to you. "At nine o'clock he was there. For a while we talked on general topics and I found that his range of knowledge was wider than many an educated man of the superior race. At last I had him tell me of himself.

"I was born," he said, "in southern Georgia. My mother was the nearly white child of a half white woman. Strange as it may seem, she was fairly well educated. By some means she had learned to read when a mere child, in the family of a man who was remarkably kind to his slaves. Later she was sold to a man whose name I can not give you, for I have heard he was my father. I can only say that he was an ambitious and intelligent man, and was afterwards governor of Georgia. Whether this man was my father or not, I do not know, but of

all his slaves none were treated with so much consideration as
my mother except me alone. He had no children by his wife,
yet he treated me more as a child than a slave, and was careful
to see that I had little to do and leisure to study and read,
which I was always eager to do. When I was fifteen I was set
free by the war and he sent me to an Ohio school. I stayed
there until his death three years ago. I am now twenty, but
compelled to make my own living, as all the large estate of
my master was taken for debt."

When he had finished, I thought for a moment, and, looking
steadily at him, I said: "Robert, how would you like to be a
white man?"

For an answer I received only an incredulous and cynical
smile. Evidently he thought I was making fun of him. I
assured him I meant what I said.

"How—what can you mean, Mr. Arnold?" he asked.

"Simply this is what I mean: I live in Minnesota. It is a
new country, settled by people from all over the world. There
you will never be taken for other than a white man, which in
reality you are. I have a law office in Minneapolis. You shall
study law under me. Later you shall be my partner. What
do you say?"

He had sprung to his feet before I finished and stood like a
man of stone. In a moment joy overspread his face and ambition gleamed in his eyes. I had not mistaken my man. There
was a deal of Anglo-Saxon blood in Robert Burton's veins.

"Oh!" he exclaimed, "how can I ever thank you? But it
can't be true. Can a man in a moment throw off the taint of
slavery, of superstition, of savagery and stand transformed and
transfigured, a man? And yet I must do it. I will, with God's
help and yours, Mr. Arnold. I'll cast aside the livery of
servitude and put on the livery of freedom. Freedom, Mr,
Arnold, means nothing unless we are peers of our fellow men.
We negroes; no, I'll not say we; but the negroes are politically
free, but are moral and social slaves. The negro in me would

sink me into slavery again, but the white blood in my veins bids me conquer and I will."

With face still beaming with such joy as can light only a freeman's countenance, he grasped my hand and wrung it in frenzied gratitude. But suddenly he dropped his head, let my hand slip from his and almost staggered to the door.

"It cannot be! Oh God! It cannot be!" he cried and hastened away.

I had entered into the plan of his becoming a freeman with almost as much enthusiasm as Robert himself. His sudden happiness was shared by me. Why he had so suddenly become downcast, I could not explain. When I saw him the next morning at his accustomed place his face bore traces of a mighty struggle. A struggle as of life and death between the superior and inferior man. I spoke to him, but made no mention of our talk the night before. All day I thought of his strange conduct and at night had reached no conclusion. I went to my room still thinking of him, when, having turned the matter over and over in my mind, I remembered that I had often seen him on the streets with a young woman, and a woman that would have been called white had one not known she had slave blood in her veins. Here then was the solution of the mystery. It was the thought of leaving her that had taken the desire for place and freedom out of him.

There was a knock at the door. In response to my invitation Robert Burton walked in. I could see at once that the struggle was still going on.

"When I left you last night, Mr. Arnold, I told you I could not go with you."

"Is love stronger than ambition?" I asked.

"Then you have guessed my secret," he exclaimed, "you have pointed out to me the path of freedom and honor, you have shown me how to cast the shackles of slavery aside. Place, fame and desire to be a man of the stature of my fellows beckon me on. But love for a woman, a woman with no more slave in her than there is in me, a love, Mr. Arnold, that is as deep as my soul, binds me in chains. How shall I decide? Shall I follow the way you have pointed out? shall I crush a heart that is full of love for me? or shall I remain as I now am, a slave? Love with bonds strong as steel binds me here, ambition with seemingly irresistable power tugs at those bonds. What shall I do, Mr. Arnold, how shall I decide?" Exhausted and in tears Robert Burton sank into a chair.

And, my reader, would you have me tell you how he decided? You know, no doubt, the power of love and it may be you know ambitions strength. Picture to yourself the difference between the honored professional man and the serving man. You could easily choose there. Imagine the pain of separating from the one dearer to you than goods or gold and the pleasure of peaceful and continued companionship with that one. Again you can decide. But if you were called to choose one and endure the other, how would you decide?

# A Little Flirt.

I met her on the cars,
  And she was fair to see;
I smiled across the seats at her,
  And she smiled back at me.

She had a jolly dimple,
  And a twinkle in her eye
That came near to being naughty,
  And that's twixt you and I.

I threw a loving kiss at her,
  While she did laugh with glee,
And from her rosy finger tips
  She tossed it back to me.

I'm heels o'er head in love with her
  As sure as I'm alive,
Although she is but three years old,
  And I am thirty-five.

## Minnehaha.

Minnehaha is a small stream near Minneapolis, Minnesota. Minnehaha Falls, a few miles east of the city, are made classically famous by Longfellow's Hiawatha. Many rich historical associations also cluster round the spot.

Here it is the first white settlers were made to run the gauntlet and here it is that not a score of years ago the primative Indians, held their war dances. The immediate surroundings have been changed into a park but the falls and the stream are the same as when Hiawatha dreamed and loved here years ago.

Minnehaha, laughing water,
  I am sitting by your side,
And I watch the crystal fountains,
  As among the rocks they glide.

O'er your falls the water's rushing,
  While I near the famous place,
And the cooling mist from off them
  Gently sprinkles in my face.

Round your falls the ivy's twining
  And the white birch gently waves,
Still the ones who loved you dearest
  Now are sleeping in their graves.

Here it was that Hiawatha,
  Dreamed of love in days gone by,
Thought of those he loved and cherished,
  Thoughts, silent thoughts, which never die.

Surely naught could be more pleasant,
  Where the sparkling water flowed,
Than to dream of absent loved ones,
  Safe in care of Him above.

'Tis no wonder Hiawatha
  Left his quiet feeding flocks,
Came to watch the laughing water,
  As it dashed among the rocks.

Minnehaha I must leave you,
  But the parting causes pain,
I like Hiawatha love you,
  Though but once your banks I've seen.

All my wandering hence may never
  Bring me back again to you,
But I'll love you ever, ever,
  *Au revoir, mais sans adieu.*

## Mammy's Boy.

"Good bye, Creston."

"Good bye, father."

It was farmer Dillon who had brought his son down to Beldan College at the beginning of the fall term in 188- . The farmer had one sunburned arm around the boy's neck as he stood on the boarding house steps bidding him good bye. Such a contrast as there was between the two: the one strong and brawny, the other pale and delicate, more like a lad from the crowded city than one from the country where scorching sun and arduous labor tend to toughen the sinews. The boy was in fact but the reflection of his invalid mother, who for years had done no other work than to aid her son in his struggle for an education. There were tears in the boy's eyes as he bade his father farewell.

"See the innocent," said one of a crowd of students lounging about the yard.

"Reckon he never was away from home before," said another.

"Mammy's boy," remarked a third, and so well to the boys' minds did this name fit the newcomer that he was afterwards known by that name alone. He was an innocent looking youth, yet withal something manly in his pale face and a more than passing intelligence in his dark eyes.

I fear he was very ignorant of college life, for when one of the boys asked him, a few days later, if he had brought his pony with him he said he had not as his father thought it would cost too much to keep it in town. And I think "cribbing" called to his mind no other performance than the work he had so often seen his father do in storing away the yearly crop of corn. When his father was gone Creston went to his room and cried himself to sleep. Foolish boy, yes but boys' hearts are tender. The next days were trying too. The new experiences, the jests of the other boys, the interminable lessons, these were the thorns in the flesh. Two weeks passed. Creston Dillon had not made many friends among the students.

"Come and have a game of cards," said Dick Braston to him one evening after supper.

"I don't play. Mother says it's wicked," was the reply.

"Mammy's boy," said Dick as he went off to find a more congenial companion. A proposal to join in a raid upon a neighboring orchard met with a similar refusal.

"I'm afraid that Dillon thinks he's just a little too good for us," commented Adrian Stanton, familiarly known to the boys as "Rex," because, I suppose, he was always ruler in any band of mischief-hunting boys of the college.

"Let's haze him," suggested Phil. Braxton.

It must have been an evil genius that put this thought into Phil's head at that particular moment. The proposition met with general approval. I would not have you think these were a lot of heartless boys. They were not, but they were sometimes thoughtless. So it was decided to haze Creston Dillon, but how were they to get hold of him? He, by some means had heard that the boys meant to haze him, and to the inexperienced boy this was supposed to be a horrible experience. He never ventured forth from his room after dark. It was Friday night the week following the raiding expedition that a crowd of boys gathered on the college campus. They were in excellent spirits and bent on having some fun.

"Now, if we only had the duffer here," said one, "we'd have some fun."

"Say boys, let's not haze that fellow. I'm afraid we'll scare him out of his wits," said Joe Barton, sometimes called tenderfoot.

"Shut up your face, kid," was Rex Stanton's answer. "It will do him good; make him tough, but then I don't see how we are to get him out," he added.

"I've got the scheme" spoke Dick Braston. "I'll go and tell

him the students are having a prayer meeting to-night and want him to come. That'll fetch the chump. Why, he reads his Bible and says his prayers every night."

"Go ahead, then," said Rex, "and don't be long, I'm aching for some fun."

The "scheme" evidently worked, for in a few minutes Dick and Creston were seen entering the campus gate. They walked on until within a few feet of a clum of elms that shaded the grounds.

"Are there many boys attend the—" Creston was saying when a half dozen boys seized him and began to tie his hands and feet.

"Don't, boys, please don't," he begged, his pale face growing paler still, and his heart beating as if it would burst his bosom.

"Keep still and it will be better for you," said Phil. Braxton. Soon they had him tied hand and foot.

"What will we do with him," asked one.

"Let's duck him in the water and cool him off," was Stanton's suggestion. "The water's getting cold now and a cold bath is good for weak people."

The crowd started off for the river, three or four of the boys carrying Creston. Of course the boys did not mean to put him in the river, but he did not know that.

"Now boys," said the leader, "I'll count three and in he goes." "Ready, one," the boy made a feeble effort to break his bonds, "two,'" a shudder ran through his frame, "three."

At three the boys made an extra effort as though they meant to cast him far into the stream, and some one threw a huge chunk of wood into the water with a splash. The boys dropped their burden to the ground. The moon strayed out from behind a cloud and shone upon the face of Creston Dillon. It was very white. "He's fainted! Bring some water, quick!" cried Rex Stanton. But mammy's boy had not fainted. He was dead. They do not haze at Beldan College now.

## Lottie Doon.

"No more the angels come to earth,"
    I've heard them say.
This was in truth my thought
        Until to-day.
But now I know they come
        A bright boon,
For I have seen thy face,
        Lottie Doon.

Not of earth were you born
        This I know.
You winged your way from heaven
        To us below.
Your smile would change e'en midnight
        Into noon.
It has banished all my sorrow,
        Lottie Doon.

There is beauty in your face,
        This is true,
But 'tis not half the beauty
        Seen in you.
Your cheeks are like the roses
        Blown in June,
Yet more beautiful your soul,
        Lottie Doon.

For your soul shines in your face
        Gladdening all,
And to worship at your feet
        I would fall.
Your pathway all through life
        Shall be strewn
Whith sweet flowers of adoration,
        Lottie Doon.

All homage you will ask
　　Shall be given,
Ere from us you shall go
　　Back to heaven.
Earth's harps will for you play
　　A glad tune,
If with us you will stay,
　　Little Doon.

## The Spring 'Neath the Old Gum Tree.

There's many a spot on the old home place,
　That I'm wishing and longing to see,
But the dearest of all is the meadow lot
　And the spring 'neath the old gum tree.

At the harvest noon when the wheat in the fields
　Waved a billowy, golden sea,
Round the clover heads the bumble bees croon
　By the spring 'neath the old gum tree.

Oh! the shade was sweet and the grass was green,
　While merry harvesters we,
Spent a happy noon hour when we used to meet
　Near the spring 'neath the old gum tree.

Then many a jest went 'round the group,
　Our hearts were happy and free.
There sang we the songs that we loved best
　By the spring 'neath the old gum tree.

The spring bubbled up with a laugh on its lips,
　And danced away to the sea;
While again and again we filled the cup
　From the spring 'neath the old gum tree.

But those days are fled in the din of life,
　And never more shall I be,
With the harvesters of then, who now are dead,
　By the spring 'neath the old gum tree.

So there's many a spot on the old home place
　That I'm wishing and longing to see,
But the dearest of all is the meadow lot
　And the spring 'neath the old gum tree.

## A Song of the Northland.

Let others sing of fair southern lands,
Where gentle breezes with lily hands
Play with the shining magnolia leaves,
Or kiss the blossoms of orange trees.

As for me, I will sing of the Northland cold,
Where men are daring and brave and bold,
And the giants come in the winter time
Bedecked with the frost of Jotunheim.

No feeling of languor pulses there;
There men are brave to do and dare,
They build not castles in idle dreams;
Their cozy homes smile when the glad sun beams.

There the blood flows quick and the heart beats fast,
And cheeks grow ruddy in wintry blast.   •
There the brain is clear and thoughts are free;
Oh, the Northland, cold and bold!
Oh! Northland cold for me!

From such a land came the Norsemen bold,
From a land of rime and frost and cold.
Forth they fared on the stormy sea,
While the storm king laughed in his savage glee.

Naught they feared from the raging sea
As forth they fared right merrily.
The strength of Winter was in their hands
And the frost bound their muscles with iron bands.

I love the Northland's winter time,
The clink of skates and the sleighbell's chime.
Let others dream 'neath the orange tree,
But the Northland, cold and bold!
Oh, Northland cold for me!

## My Rival.

"Are you sure you love only me, my darling?"

"Yes, only you, and you with all my heart."

I was bidding sweet Edena good night. I had just proposed to her and been accepted. She formed a beautiful picture as she stood there on the step in the milky moonlight, her beautiful hair, wavy as the silk upon the corn, falling carelessly around her fair neck and shoulders. My heart beat a love rhyme as I looked upon her.

In my long acquaintance with Edena I had never known her to tell me other than the truth. How could I know that the soul that looked out of those eyes, sparkling, as I thought, with love, was that of an Annanias? She had said that she loved me and I believed it. Oh, the cruel time when I was undeceived! But let me not too soon tell my story.

Edena had promised that she would be my wife and I was very happy. During our courtship I had been a frequent caller at her home. After our engagement I went more often. Time glided by in his golden wheeled chariot and almost a year had passed since our engagement. I felt confident that I still held first place in my love's heart. The time for our wedding was but two weeks off.

I had been busy in my office all day, and in the evening sought the home of my sweetheart, anticipating a pleasant time. Then it was I first saw my rival. He sat calmly on the sofa beside Edena where I had so often sat. She rose and gave me a kiss of greeting, but he, curse him, made no sign of giving me his place. Edena again took her seat beside him. I flung myself into a rocker and tried to ignore his presence. But I could not talk. Jealousy was continually biting my heart. It is a soul-trying position to be with the one you love and that in the presence of one you hate with all the bitterness of your nature. I could not make myself agreeable, and though it was only occasionally that my love deigned to notice my rival with some remark, I grew angrier every minute.

In an hour I asked for my hat and overcoat and started home. Edena saw that I was troubled and asked the cause. I made some evasive answer, and as I went out at the door I cast a malignant glance back at him who I thought was trying to rob me of my heart's treasure. His answering look was one of confident insolence. A formal handshake and a coldly spoken good night was the only parting I took of Edena that evening. I usually kissed her affectionately at parting, but to-night my lips felt cold as ice and I was sensible of a feeling of repugnance for her, as I thought perhaps she had lately kissed another.

When I reached my room I could not sleep. Had there been ten thousand demons in my bed they could not have tormented me more than did that single gnawing, jealous feeling. Morning came and I went to my work with a heavy heart. My thoughts continually reverted to the parlor where I had spent the evening before, and all the while the face of my rival came up before me like a hateful vision in a sweet dream. To love and to know that one is loved: O, how it lightens the labors of life! But to be jealous and hate, burns one to cinder. When evening came my anguish was unbearable and I determined to go again to Edena, tell her my feelings and ask her to choose between us. I of course expected to find her alone. What was my chagrin when upon again entering the parlor I saw my rival in the same place—once mine—as he had had the evening before. My soul rose up in protest. I felt like turning upon my heel and leaving at once. I sat down, however, in a chair and tried to start up a conversation.

It seemed to me that Edena was not near so lavish of her attention to me as she used to be, while more and more, as I fancied, she gave attention to my rival. Every word she spoke to him made my heart beat more angrily and my breath come harder. But Edena seemed not to mind. She continued her attention to him, seeing, as I thought, that it taunted me. Suddenly, as if to insult me more deeply, she placed her arms around his neck and before my very face kissed him!

This was more than I could brook. My face flamed and my eyelids trembled with anger. I jumped up from my seat and grasped my hat and started for the door.

"Edena," cried I, as I paused a moment at the threshold, "Fare you well. I believed you loved me, me only. I have been deceived. May I never look upon your face again."

"O, Jerald!" she exclaimed, springing to her feet and casting him from her arms, "What is the matter with you?"

I made an effort to go, but her velvety arms were around my neck. I thought of the night I stood on the steps—the night after our engagement. I thought how beautiful she was then. She was more beautiful now. I did not mean to do it, but some irresistable power made me print a kiss on her soft cherry lips. Her arms came tighter around my neck. Then I wondered if I had not been very foolish to be so jealous—yes, so jealous—of only a pug.

# In West Virginia.

In West Virginia skies are blue,
The hills are green and hearts are true;
A joyous welcome waiteth you,
    In West Virginia.

In West Virginia skies are bright,
The twinkling stars make glad the night;
And noble hearts uphold the right,
    In West Virginia.

In West Virginia, happy beams
The sun that kisses crystal streams,
Enduring love is what it seems,
    In West Virginia.

In West Virginia there is rest
For tempest-tossed and sore distressed.
Here loving hearts are ever blest,
    In West Virginia.

In West Virginia man is free;
He dwells beneath his own roof-tree;
Oh come, my love, and dwell with me,
    In West Virginia.

## Recollections of An Old Bachelor.

An old bachelor, to the minds of many, is a useless but necessary evil. Something not unendurable, yet not to be admired.
He is considered as something left over, a by-product of the
refining processes of society, as it were. His heart must of
course be of marble, travertine or some like substance, else he
had long ago succumbed to the circumventive wiles of some
fair charmer and would now have a band of tiny prattlers
around his knee. His lot (provided he owns a trap and fine
horses) will not be entirely desolate. Many will be the girls
who will vote him awful nice because he has taken them on a
pleasant trip, and he will receive many a smile as he drives
along the street lifting his hat—a shining bald head coming
into view as he does so—to those fair ones who lean out of the
window to see him pass.

Then he will have the pleasure of introducing the debutantes
into the circle of society. He used to be a beau of their mamma's and is and old friend of the family, you know. Besides
all this he furnishes a haven of rest for the half dozen old
maids of the village, who have either wrecked their affections
upon some heartless wretch, or else, for reasons best known to
themselves, have never set out on the sea of love, whose shores
are banked with roses and whose isles yield the perfume of the
orange blossom, yet in whose depths are dark and hidden
wrecking rocks. For these, I say, he is a source of comfort,
for his heart stretched by the expanding influence of many
loves is ample for them all, and then he is about their age and
*might* get married.

He is likely to be a good talker and could tell many a strange
tale if he would about his adventures in divers parts of the
world; for he has traveled far and wide and has seen the *bon
ton* of Paris.

As I sit in my room this winter's evening with my feet to the
fire, and as the winds hold a howling concert on the outside,

my thoughts turn inward and I hold a reverie with myself. My pipe has sent my brain into a half dreamland, and as the rings of smoke curl up from it I see strange—not strange, but almost forgotten faces—framed in its wreaths. There is a little golden-haired girl of four or five, and she smiles at me shyly. Ah, where have I seen that face? I remember now, but she has vanished. In that wider ring I see another face; this time the hair is dark and the eyes have a womanly look. There is a meaning in those eyes, though they have dwelt upon the beauties of but sixteen summers. I think I know the face; let me look again—pshaw! it has disappeared and another takes its place. A woman, this; and from a wreath of smoke a mass of dark brown curls fall out and a pair of big, brown eyes gaze with no unfriendly meaning into my face. I will speak to her, but—she is gone.

Here no wreath of smoke, only a huge cloud of it, but in that cloud I see a pair of eyes—fascinatingly dark and dangerous. A face of a rosy-cheeked, dark brunette is half visible through the smoke. In an instant another, very like the first, appears beside it. I feel my heart beat quickly as I look upon these beautiful visions. Which is the most beautiful? A heart rending cry of pain caused me to drop my pipe and I awoke startled from my dream.

I felt a knife; it seemed to graze my cheek. I put my hand to my face. Yes, there was an ugly cut, but it was long ago healed and nothing but the scar remained. I then knew I had been in a land of dreams and not one of realities. But what of the faces I had seen? Ah, they were those of persons closely linked with my life.

## Shooting Stars.

(From the French of Beranger.)

Shepherd, say you that in the skies
  Gleams the star that guides our sail?
'Tis so, my child, but from our eyes
  Night hides that star within her veil.
Shepherd, 'tis thought with mystic arts
  You read the secret of the skies;
What is that star that downward darts,
  Which darts, darts and darting dies?

My child, an erring mortal dies,
  And instant downward shoots his star.
He drank and sang amid the cries
  Of friends whose joys no hatred mars.
Happy he sleeps, nor moves nor starts,
  After the wine he quiet lies—
Another star is seen which darts,
  Which darts, darts and darting dies.

My child, see that one pure and sweet,
  A lovely vision, charming all,
A faithful bride, 'tis well and meet
  Her lover leads her from the ball.
Flowers bind her brow with skillful arts
  And spread the marriage feast now lies—
Behold! a beauteous star which darts,
  Which darts, darts and darting dies.

My son, you see that flashing light?
  'Tis of a great lord new to earth.
The cradle vacant from his flight
  Was decked with purple at his birth.
The poisons sold in flattery's marts
  Appeased his hunger, hushed his cries—
'Tis but another star which darts,
  Which shooting, darts and darting dies.

My child, behold that sinister spark,
  A cherished favorite's guiding star,
Who thought it was the great man's mark
  To laugh at ills that others mar.
By those who bowed with servile hearts
  His image now all shattered lies,
Another star which earthward darts,
  Which darts, darts and darting dies.

And lo! that of the mighty czar!
  But go, my son, guard well the truth,
Nor empty glitter mark your star
  In childhood's days or riper youth.
If no use marks your brilliant part,
  The world will say and pass you by:
"He's like the gleaming stars which dart,
  Which dart, dart and darting die."

## The Revelation of Harry Sheldon.

"Girls," said Clara Rich, "come round to my room this evening and we will get our Latin lessons out together."

"All right, Clara," said Bessie Barton, one of the three girls addressed, "we'll be there."

All these girls were students in a co-educational college in one of the southern states, and a bright set of girls they were, too. Don't picture to yourself a group of old maids, for our laughing young friends were not that; only four jolly girls who had graduated from the village high school the year before and were now treading the thorny path that only the freshman knows.

I did not say the girls were pretty. You of course know that much; for in the wide realm who ever saw a high-school graduate that was not.

As this, however, is not to be a love story—oh do not lay the book down so spitefully, my dear young lady—I will not dwell upon the charms of their sweet faces, though I have it on good authority that their appearance in college in the fall term was responsible for a certain almost bald old bachelor senior appearing regularly thereafter in a clean cravat; a thing he had always scorned.

But to my story. The girls met at Clara's home at the appointed hour. "Did you ever see such a lesson as that old crank gave us?" spoke out Jessie Stanton.

"No, nor anybody else," approved Pearl Spence.

"Girls," said Clara Rich, "I don't think it's one bit of harm to read with a pony when the teacher gives us such a long lesson."

Yes, I must give these dear searchers for knowledge away. They had all come to Clara's home that they might have the use of her interlinear to untangle the *dignus vindice nodus.* I am sorry to have to put this indictment on paper, but then they were only human, and besides it is a part of the story.

The paraphernalia is all at hand, a dictionary, several texts with notes, and then that interlinear which bore a white paper cover on which some hand—feminine I fear—had carefully lettered "Hymns and Psalms." All went well for awhile, but then the labor languished for a season, and the conversation turned upon the boy students in general, and one Harry Sheldon, a studious, quiet fellow, in particular.

"He studies too much and never looks at the girls," said Bessie.

"Just a little slow and a trifle green, I think," added Pearl.

"He's too good to read from a translation, I bet," put in Jessie.

What more they would have said I don't know, but looking out of the parlor window just at that moment they saw him coming up through the yard.

"There he comes now," said Clara, looking up, "and now we can't use our"——but he had rung the doorbell and she hastened to answer it.

"Girls," said Harry, I saw you all come in here with your books and I thought I would come over and study with you. It's dreadful lonesome in my room. No harm done I hope."

"Oh, we are glad to see you, indeed," said Pearl as she slipped the interlinear further under the sofa cushion, "you can help us."

They chatted a few minutes and then went at the Odes with a vengeance. They rolled along famously with the first one, and the second made good sense, but the third seemed to have wrapped up in it the diabolical instincts of all the Romans and was as untranslatable as the veriest Choctaw.

For half an hour they struggled with it. Three-quarters and no satisfactory results. The girls were ready to cry. Harry was half mad.

"I have a little book here that sometimes I use under very trying circumstances," and with this he drew out "Horace's Complete Works—A Translation."

The girls were astonished, he did it so deliberately.   But at heart they rejoiced, just as all sinners do when they find others committing their faults.   Then there was light where before was obscurity, and the third Ode was mastered.

"Well, good-bye, girls," spoke Harry, donning his cap and taking his book he went whistling home.

"Isn't he just lovely," asserted Jessie.   If there was a dissenting voice to this verdict it never reached my ears.

## Noel.

'Tis Christmas time and we hear the chime
  Of the sleigh bells' tinkling steel.
'Tis Christmas tide and we give our gifts
  To show the love we feel.

## Books.

In books I hold sweet converse
   With those mighty souls,
That beat their being out
   Uron this shore.

Their thoughts more precious
   Than the precious gold,
Are here heaped up for me
   In bounteous store.

# A Rondolet.

Dear sweet Jeanette
  With glances coy and laughing eyes.
My sweet Jeanette,
I feel your heaving bosom yet,
Your kisses warm as a sunny day,
Your throbbing heart so near mine lay,
My dear Jeanette.

Dear sweet Jeanette,
With glances coy and laughing eyes.
My sweet Jeanette,
What dimpled cheeks and tresses jet.
How swift the winged hour flies;
When on my bosom your head lies.
My dear Jeanette.

## The Mysterious Brooch.

One evening two years ago I sat talking with my friend, Frank LeFeever, in his cosy room in the Latin Quarter in Paris. LeFeever was an artist, a Frenchman by birth and culture, and I suppose would have been classed by Herr Nordeau as a degenerate, so strongly did the beautiful affect him. But our talk was not of philosophers or degenerates; it was of the thousand and one things that may be gossipped about in the gay and flashing French capital. The whirl and swirl, the gaudiness and giddiness of this metropolis had made a powerful impression on me—a graduate of one of the smaller colleges of the United States who had come over to polish himself off and see a bit of life. Here in this part of the city, eminently the home of students, I found the companions and entertainment best suited to my taste and financial status. How I made the acquaintance of LeFeever is of little importance. He was my room-mate at my landlady's, and though I at first felt a peculiar aversion for him I came to like him more as time passed, and now after three months I felt a real union with him. There was nothing peculiarly attractive about him, nor on the other hand was there anything to cause positive dislike. He was about twenty-eight, five years older than myself.

His shoulders were slightly stooped, his hair was thin and light in color, his face was pale and angular, and his eyes were the blue that one so often sees in the half obscured skies in Indian summer.

His expression was sad and sometimes his absent-mindedness seem to approach idiocy. At first I thought that his severe studies in art and his continual labor with chisel and brush were proving too much for him, and that his mind was giving way under the strain.

His talk, however, was of the most rational sort, and his actions, with one exception, those of a perfectly sane man. I concluded at last that these spells of absorbing absent-mindedness were the result of some great and deep shadows of sorrow that had crossed his life. I spoke of one peculiar action. It had to do with an old leather pocketbook which he guarded with care, as if it contained some priceless treasure. Every night on going to bed he placed it under his pillow. On awakening the first thing he did was to put it in the pocket of the coat he expected to wear that day. Once or twice, when he thought I was not looking, I saw him take some shining object out, press it to his lips and replace it with as much tenderness as if it had been some living being capable of feeling pain. At other times he would rivet his eyes upon the seemingly insignificant object as if it were some powerful spiritual magnet from which he could not wrest away his soul. I felt a real sorrow for such a brilliant mind, so near, as I thought, to the verge of insanity.

I shall not forget the night in question when we sat each with a cigarette between his lips. Our conversation at last turned to theaters, and we spoke of the noted Spanish singer Otero, who was to be heard at the Academie de Musique on the following night. "Of course we shall go," said LeFeever. "I bought two tickets today and want you to accompany me." I readily assented.

"Where are our seats?" I asked.

"I have forgotten," replied my companion, "but can tell you in a minute as I have the tickets with me."

He drew from his pocket the old leather pocketbook which I have mentioned and proceeded to search for them.

They were deep in one of the pockets of the purse, and as he gave it a shake to get at them a beautiful gold brooch fell out and rolled across the floor. I rose from my chair and stooped to get it for him, but just as I did this he struck me a blow with his fist that sent me staggering to the corner.

"For God sake, man, what do you mean!" I cried. I looked at him: his face was pale as death. His right hand clasped the shining brooch as in death agony: his left was on his heart.

*O mon dieu! mon coeur!* he shrieked and fell fainting to the floor.

I lifted him up and laid him on the bed. In a few moments he gained consciousness. He still held the treasured object in his hand and hastened to place it in the old purse. Then he looked up at me with such an expression of sorrow and sadness as would have melted a heart harder than mine. "I beg you forgive me, Harmer," said he, "and as you respect me as a friend, say nothing of this."

I gave him my promise and he turned his face, yet deathly pale, to the wall and went to sleep.

The next day he went to his work half heartedly, and at night seemed anxious for eight o'clock to come that he might go to the theater. The streets were a living sea of people, and as we passed through the crowd I noticed that LeFeever kept his hand over the left breast of his gilet, in the inner pocket of which I knew he carried the mysterious piece of jewelry which seemed to have such a strange power over him.

We found the theater packed. It was a great event. The first time Otero had ever sung in Paris. Her fame was well established in Spain and now she was starting on a tour of the world. The orchestra played some moving airs which set one's pulses faster beating. The whole audience was on the *qui vive* and expectant. I looked at my companion. His face was beaming with pleasure, and I knew his rare artistic nature expected a treat.

The curtain rang up and a wave of excitement spread over the immense crowd and all leaned forward in eager expectancy. LeFeever was no less eager than the rest. I was glad he had apparently forgotten the unpleasant circumstance of the previous night. Immediately Otero stepped forward. A true type of Spanish beauty. Dark features boldly outlined; deep, dark eyes, capable of love and vengeance; a well formed woman whose head was crowned with luxuriant, black, raven hair. Such was the famous singer. She stepped forward with conscious pride. There was an uproar of applause. When this died away a shriek, as of a demon, at my side, caused me to stare in amazement at LeFeever, who was standing upright in his seat. There was a look of murder in his eyes. His face was fixed* and hard. Before I could recover sufficiently from my surprise to speak to him he leaped into the aisle and started for the stage. In one hand he grasped tightly the leather pocketbook, ragged and worn; in the other gleamed a bright new dagger. So complete was the surprise of the whole audience that he had almost reached the stage before two gensdarmes seized him.

"You assassin," he cried, and tried to climb upon the stage, but the officers held him back.

At the sound of his voice Otero gave a shriek and fled behind the wings of the stage.

The next morning the papers bore in bold headlines, "A MAD MAN IN A THEATRE."

# Le Feever's Confession.

## Sequel to the Mysterious Brooch.

A fortnight had elapsed since the memorable night at the theater and I had not seen Le Feever. I was in my room closely intent upon one of Villon's poems, endeavoring to have some definite image called up by his mystic thoughts. There came a light knock on the door, and upon my invitation Le Feever walked in. His face, even paler than usual, lighted up perceptibly at my warm greeting, and after bidding me good evening he sat down. I had read in that evening's paper that after a careful examination the doctors had failed to discover any traces of insanity in Le Feever, and consequently he had been released. For this reason his visit was no great surprise. I could not help but notice that he was ill at ease—the uneasiness which possesses a man who guards some great secret which he can no longer keep to himself. I spoke to him on various topics, endeavoring to engage him in conversation, but my attemps were futile and he grew more and more restless. At last he arose, walked to the window and gazed into the street, drumming meanwhile idly with his fingers on the pane. Then he turned and came to a stand directly in front of me, and placing his hand upon my shoulder looked straight into my face.

"Yes, I think I can trust you," he began abruptly. "Harmer, after the peculiar actions you have seen in me you must consider me either a fool or a mad man."

I made some evasive answer, but he went on:

"I now mean to confide to you a secret which if you will keep, and lend me your sympathy and help, may be the means of saving me; but if you fail, God help me and you too, for I will take your life."

I made him a solemn promise to guard his secret and do anything honorable in my power to help him.

"You have wondered," he then resumed, "why so insignificant a thing as a gold brooch could have such an influence on a man's life. I will tell you, Harmer. The most simple things may have such a meaning attached to them by association that they will ruin weak men and make strong men turn pale. Such a meaning has that piece of jewelry for me. But to my story: If ever man loved, I loved Viviane Fincelle. We had been child, youthful, and full-grown lovers. Her father, a merchant of considerable means, had taken a liking to me on account of my artistic talent, and did not scorn me because I was poor. Viviane and I were engaged to be married in one year, after I was of age. This year I decided to spend in travel and chose a journey through Spain, cursed country of legend and superstition and jealousy that it is. I started in March and by June I had found a beautiful little town among the foot hills of the Cantabrian mountains. Here at Bolano I decided to spend some weeks in sketching and in the meantime to make my home with Senor Vasquez, the only hotel keeper in the place. The entertainment at his place was not of the highest order but it was the best there. In the Vasquez family, numerous though it was, there was but one person for whom I formed a liking. This was his daughter Delmonte, a typical Spanish girl of seventeen, in whom the animal and the beautiful far outshone any mental culture she possessed. The blood in my veins was warm and soon we were desperately in love, as flirtation love goes. She was my companion and hindrance in the foot tours I took over the hills near the town on those beautiful Spanish summer days. She grew more and more fond of me with that love which flashes into hate in an instant. I became more and more interested in her. Of an evening we would sit together beneath the garden arbor, and while I talked

to her of painting and art she would twine her arms around
my neck and punctuate my sentences with kisses. Thus we
spent some weeks, and I was in no hurry to leave my hospita-
ble guest nor his pretty daughter. On returning one evening
from one of my daily strolls I was told that some new guests
had arrived. Upon entering the hotel parlor I was surprised
to greet Viviane Fincelle and her father. They had started on
a journey to Rome, two months after I had left for
my summer's trip, but had decided to loiter along through
Spain on their way thither. It was by good fortune we
had met,

Of course I was glad to see the girl I loved above above
everything else in the world, and my Senorita was soon forgotten when Viviane said she and her father expected to remain a week at Bolano. But a Spanish love dies not easily;
or if it dies, unconquerable hate springs from its lifeless body
as the new polyp from the dead shell. Delmonte did not
forget. She watched Viviane with jealous eyes, for she was
now my companion in my rambles. I sometimes fancied I saw
the image of the devil of hate reflected in Delmonte's eyes.
She said nothing, but on the altar of her heart smouldered the
fire ready for a horrible sacrifice to the God of jealousy. And
she was priestess at that sacrifice. One evening after the day's
tramping, Viviane and I sat under the arbor where I so often
had sat with the Spanish girl. Over us hung large clusters of
grapes which glinted purple in the setting sun. Away on the
hills we heard the tripping tinkle of the sheep bells, the whis-
tle of the shepherd and the bark of his dog. In the trees
around the insects hummed and drummed the sleepy tunes they
learned when the world was young. I had been telling to
Viviane how dearer to me than all else was she. Blushingly
she had heard it and rose to pluck a delicious bunch of grapes.
Leaning over the back of the rustic seat, one hand on my
shoulder, she gave them to me. I looked up into her face.
She was supremely happy. I drew her down and kissed her

lips. At that instant there was a rustling noise, the vines parted. I saw the bright gleam of a dagger, there was a death shriek and a gush of blood flowed over me and trickled down my bosom. Viviane, my love, my love, my all, fell limp across my shoulder gasping, dying, the life blood pouring from a wound on the side of her neck.

As I sat thus in the dumbness of heart which comes to one who feels he has lost all except his own life, which he most desires to loose, something bright fell from my dying Viviane's throat into my lap. "This is it," said Le Feever, choking with grief, as he held up the mysterious brooch, "and Otero of the Music Hall is Delmonte Vasquez."

I looked at the brooch closely; its underside was stained with blood.

# A Song of Today.

Come fill up the cup to the brim, to the brim,
And we'll drink a health to him, to him,
Who toils all day in the heat and sun,
And saith at night, "my work is done."

Great sweat-beads stand on his face, his face,
Where days of toil have left their trace, their trace.
His hands are rough and his arms are brown,
But his head doth richly deserve the crown

Of honest worth.   Today he asks for bread, for bread;
His brother gives him stone instead, instead.
A stone, a stone is his for bread,
His brother giveth a stone instead.

## Selections from Abdiolel. *

I know 'tis said that cruel death
  Is anxious for a shining mark;
Certes he found it when the spark
  Of thy young life went out with breath.

But why at thee this foe so fell
  So soon should aim his fatal dart,
Which cruel pierced thy youthful heart,
  Is more than thy weak friend can tell.

   *    *    *    *    *

And does he mark with ill intent
  Those who mount upward as the flame,
And soon would grasp a place from fame,
  With which they well might rest content?

   *    *    *    *    *

But we are taught that over all
  There ruleth one Almighty Lord,
Without whose knowledge and whose word,
  May not a single sparrow fall.

All are subject to His command—
  The dreaded powers of lasting night,
The shining ones of blessed light,
  Alike are governed by His hand.

That in his wisdom what He doth,
  Is best for those who trust his name,
Though at the first faith's flickering flame
  Does not give light to see it thus.

So unto him this dreaded death
  Must then be subject with the rest,
And can but act at His behest
  When He does take a mortal's breath.

* Note. –The lines under this head are in memory of my friend and classmate,
Lawrence S. Maulsby. They are taken from Abdiolel, a poem written while I was in
California and published in pamphlet form September, 1894.

If thus I learn, I must allow
  That e'en the death of my dear friend
Will be my profit in the end,
  However much I sorrow now.

    *     *     *     *     *

When sorrow's angry clouds hang low,
  And deluge our poor souls with grief,
O send us quickly Thy relief,
  That we may all Thy goodness know.

'Tis when across our hearts are made
  The furrows misery's ploughshare turns,
When all we've loved or trusted spurns,
  We turn to Thee and ask Thine aid.

    *     *     *     *     *

Yet help us still in our distress,
  Around us place Thy shielding power,
That we may learn each day and hour
  To love Thee more and fear Thee less.

    *     *     *     *     *

I seem to hear the scoffer laugh
  When God or Heaven to him are named,
For those he seemeth much ashamed
  Who found their hopes upon such chaff.

He fain would have us all believe
  There is no Heaven, there is no God;
No bright reward, no chastening rod,
  But all are visions which deceive.

    *     *     *     *     *

Are we but cunning casts in clay?
  Fashioned by the hand of chance,
And on us will there never glance
  The beamings of a brighter day?

### THE ROSE OF SHARON.

Neath Judean suns 'twas planted,
  In the ages past away,
Beat about by persecution,
  Growing stronger every day.

Not uprooted by man's anger,
    Nor scorched midst martyr flames,
Ever greater grow its branches,
    Bearing many noble names.

Down the centuries ran its rootlets,
    Twining midst the misty years.
Shading every clime and people,
    By its verdure, from their tears.

And I look adown the future,
    'Long Time's gliding river's shore,
And I see the Rose of Sharon
    Blooming brightly evermore.

\*    \*    \*    \*

None would deny that men of greed,
    In ages past, mid many climes,
Did deeds of death and bloody crimes,
    And claimed the Bible as their creed.

\*    \*    \*    \*

So thus they wrought 'neath sunny clime,
    Until the Rome which Peter gave
Made man a seven-fold more slave
    Than did the Cæsars in their prime.

\*    \*    \*    \*

We should not for what is false
    Reject alike what's good and true,
And say that naught is pure we view,
    That all is sin and wicked all.

From out the mass of useless chaff
    Let us with patience take the grain,
Though winnowing cause us toil and pain,
    Our work will speak in our behalf.

Old feudal castles covered o'r with moss
    Should not for that command respect,
Nor men who say they're God's elect,
    If all their works consist of dross.

Whate'er has aided man to climb
From out a rude and savage life,
Away from evil, sinful strife,
May truthfully be called divine.

Scatter creeds to earth's four winds,
And may the blast that leaves no trace,
Roll back the clouds which hide God's face,
That we may know His laws, not man's.

If all the creeds that man has made
Were lost in one consuming blaze,
Right would be right in every phase,
And good be good as ever staid.

I hold it true what I believe
Is of less worth than what I do.
I may believe that which is true
And do the acts that all deceive.

\*        \*        \*        \*

Not what we think or yet profess
Makes up the sum of our brief lives,
But what man does; for what he strives
Will sadly curse or gladly bless.

But let me rest and sweet repose
Steal calmly o'er my troubled heart,
And soothe me with the healing art
That honest toil and labor knows.

Sweet recollection bodies forth the forms
Of pleasures past, of joyous ties,
I've known e'er this neath other skies
Before for him I came to mourn.

Once more I'm sitting in the wood,
Where glides the silver stream along:
Once more I hear the Spring's glad song,
She sings to give us happy mood.

## SPRING'S SONG.

Down in the valley the violets are springing,
Overhead in the trees the blue bird is singing,
The heart of the phœbe is warmed by the sun,
And out of his throat sweet music doth run.
Through the grass glides the snake,
Mother Nature's awake.

Sweet little anemone up on the hill,
Jolly young buttercup down by the rill,
Are laughing and singing all the day long,
While the frisky young daises dance to their
    song;
The grass is a carpet under our feet,
And all things are sweet.

Hear the cock crowing,
Hear the herds lowing,
Hear the quail calling far 'gainst the hill,
And his mate's answer soft and still.
See the maize springing.
And robin swinging
Gayly near by on the apple tree bough;
E'en the sad sparrow is happy now.

The sturdy woodpecker, a carpenter he,
Is busily pounding the old oak limb,
Making a house for his wife and him;
    While the bee,
    In days that are sunny,
    He gathers his honey
    For the cold, cold time
    When the sleghbells chime.

Beautiful butterfly of gaudy wing,
Short-lived heralder of spring,
Alights on the poppy to rest,
And thinks how best
He may show his beauty,
Scarce thinks he of duty.

Let the birds sing,
And joyous ring;
'Tis the glad time of Spring,
When from their graves
Creep the flowers and the leaves
To gladden our hearts once more,
Our hearts that are sore.

   *       *       *       *       *       *

Awaked!  O can it be that what I saw
  And what I heard was but a dream?
And so it was, though it doth seem
  Too real to own the slightest flaw.

Strange power of mind that in the night
  Brings former scenes to us again.
Oh that they might with us remain,
  And never vanish from our sight.

'Tis long now since that happy day
  I sat with him 'neath shady trees.
And heard Spring's music in the breeze,
  Yet seemeth it but yesterday.

Time's swift wheeled chariot moves along,
  And leaves behind the dust of years,
Which dust is mingled with the tears
  Wrung from all men, however strong.

Again has come the smiling year;
  Once more I hear the blue bird sing,
'Tis but a year since last 'twas spring,
  Yet not such music sweet I hear.

It seemeth time is out of tune,
  Or striketh not the chords aright.
Across my soul hath come a blight,
  I feel aweary much too soon.

Weary and I know not why;
  'Tis not with labor's heavy task;
Yet scarce the reason need I ask,
  I live 'neath sorrow's clouded sky.

But those who see me in the crowd,
  Say, "Naught of sorrow hath he known.
By him the happy years have flown
  With joyous song and laughter loud."

'Tis true I am but slight of years;
  Just through life's book begun to leaf;
But this I know, that extreme grief
  Locks up the fountain of our tears.

  *  *  *  *  *  *

Once more the flowers bloom on the hills.
  The birds that singing in the trees
Fling music on the fitful breeze
  That flutters by the dancing rills.

Borne along by the south wind
  Comes Spring to gladden every one,
With subtle warmth of mellowing sun,
  That lends the earth its beamings kind.

But there's a heart twelve months ago
  Beat happily with Spring's caress,
That beats no more; it is at rest,
  Sleeping where blue violets grow.

The Spring that him much pleasure gave,
  With singing birds in every tree;
That blossomed flowers for him to see,
  Can now but blow one on his grave.

And yet the springtime giveth hope,
  With springing flowers and budding leaves.
The swallows building 'neath the eaves
  Cheer us who in the darkness grope.

Whence came the flowers sprung up by earth?
  From her cold bosom, brown and bare,
To scatter fragrance on the air,
  What was the power that wiled them forth?

And what the Power that from the bud
  Could shape in beauty the green leaf?

  *  *  *  *  *  *

A simple seed a flower may be,
    That springing upward from the ground.
Will sweeten, gladden all around,
    And let us all its beauty see.

'Tis true we see the seeds no more,
    Nor could we wish it, since the flower
Hath brought us many a happy hour.
    That we had never known before.

The simple seed contains the life,
    Yet it must perish ere we see
The lovely flower or beauteous tree,
    Or we can learn that it has life.

    *      *      *      *      *      *

Hear the hail upon the roofs,
Like the horses' horny hoofs,
Beating on the frozen ground,
All around, up and down
Are the dancers in white gown.

Merry hail from the clouds,
Coming down dressed in shrouds
    Of pure white,
Were you not afraid to fall?
Down from Heaven's high blue wall
    Did it you affright?

Drops of hail in your shrouds,
Will you ever reach the clouds
    Once again?
Yes, the sun will carry us back
On his shoulders broad, alack;
    In good time.

The clouds hang low as if they came
Anxious to bring the rain:
But old Aeolus blew his breath
Cold and caused the raindrops death;
And the hail now so white,
Dancing on the roof thus light;
Is the rain in winding sheet,

Even death may be sweet.

\* \* \* \* \*

The rugged quartz contains the gold,
Yet must be crushed ere we can gain,
The beauteous, glistening, golden grain,
To cast into the glowing mold.

In gazing on the mighty weight
Is used to crush the rugged rock,
One can but think the heavy shock
Will waste the precious gold complete.

But 'tis the rock alone is lost,
Returning to the mother earth,
And all that is of any worth
Is brought out shining, free from dross.

So when the heavy stamp of death
Doth crush to earth this mound of clay,
It does but gently ope the way
And give a deathless spirit breath.

\* \* \* \* \*

No life is vain that does a deed
Of kindness to some mortal here,
That cheers a heart or dries a tear,
Or aids poor struggling mankind's need.

\* \* \* \* \*

The twig that's burdened with a weight,
The floweret trampled in the dust,
The grain stalk blighted with a rust
Can ne'er be beautiful or straight.

\* \* \* \* \*

The crowning beauty of the rose
But hides the thorns upon its stem,
Who plucks the rose is pricked by them
Ere it another parent knows.

If on the rose stem was no thorn,
If we might pluck it free from pain,

Then we would count it little gain
    To hold a flower so poor, forlorn.

\*        \*        \*        \*

Come, Memory, take me by the hand
    And lead me thither once again,
Unto those scenes I so well ken,
    Though now I tread a foreign strand.

\*        \*        \*        \*        \*

But should I chance into the town,
    And should I pass again the street,
Where oft we trod with joyous feet
    And gladsome wandered up and down,

And should I meet him in the mart,
    Should he to me his hand extend,
I'd grasp it firmly and my friend
    Embrace without a startled heart.

I could not deem it very strange,
    Should I thus meet him in the way,
Where passed us many a happy day,
    Gone now from this life's narrow range.

\*        \*        \*        \*        \*

I love to wander out and be alone with Mother Nature:
She charms me with her quiet solitude,
And her birds and rippling streams make music
Sweeter far than any instrument of man's invention.
How great she seems, and I how small.
It seemeth meet that I should bow and offer praise
To Him who in His might hath reared
These hills and hung in space this swinging sphere.
Can he not guide the fragile bark of my poor soul
Throughout the tempest tossings of this world,
And bring me safe at last into the port,
When life's brief voyage is at end?

\*        \*        \*        \*

I'll break from off my weeping, no longer I'll mourn.
In silence and sadness my grief I have borne,
In these stranded cries, but pulsations of grief

My heart has sought refuge, my soul found relief,
The affection I bore him these measures beat out;
Now hoping, now trusting, now deluged in doubt.
Oft by faith laying hold on Heaven's high throne:
Oft wandering in darkness, untrusting, alone.
And crossing sometimes the cold borders of death,
In fancy imagined that I felt the breath
Of the breezes, made fragrant with sweet odors rife,
Caught while tossing the branches of the glad tree of life.
With feet yet unholy I've trod streets of gold,
Searching Heavenly mansions his face to behold.
I have heard joyous music, such as angels can play,
Who bask in the sunshine of eternal day.
You may call this a vision, you may call it a dream,
As idle as murmur of pure purling stream.
Ah so it may be, but I think it not so;
I deem them vibrations of a heart filled with woe.

## The Lost Child.

*The following lines are founded upon a real incident which occurred a few years ago in California, among the Sierra Nevada mountains.*

O listen to that mother's cry;
  It seems that it will pierce
The very hearts of sturdy pines,
  It rings so loud and fierce.

What a wail, O God! the cause
  Is told in that continued shriek:
"My child is lost! my child is *lost!*
  God give me strength! I faint; I'm weak!"

The pines make no reply, but moan;
  They seem to grieve in sympathy.
Sierra's peaks rise dark around and seem to say:
  "We hide thy child from thee."

'Tis so; the searchers wander, dark the way.
  So near they once the little wanderer came
They heard her sob and breathe;
  They called, it frightened her away—her name.

They stretch their hands, the gloom
  Was all they felt. Not there;
She'd fled. A tiny track or two
  Shown by a match's glare.

Continued search. The same
  Results. Day by day they strive.
O'er and o'er the searchers ask:
  "Dead or alive? Dead or alive?"

"Mangled, crushed, torn, or yet all safe?
  Cast down from some high place?
Killed by some beast? Perhaps well;
  'Twould be a comfort but to see her face."

Hid in some covert; fearing those
  Who mean her only good?
Thinking them savages, to escape
  Fleeing to a deeper wood?

Night again.   Distraction, pain
  For that poor mother.   God sustain
And comfort her.   Help her bear up
  In this sad hour when sorrows reign.

The search is o'er.   Found? Yes.
  "Lifeless or with breath?"   Dread
Silence.   Tread softly.   In a mountain pool,
  'Mid crystal waters—found—dead.

## Them Frogs.

Listen to them frogs down there in the pond;
Haint nothin' on earth that I'm quite as fond
Of hearin' as them same frogs.   When I hear
Them croakin' I'm just sure spring's near.

When they begin it kinder sets me to wishin'
That I had some bait an' that old fishin'
Pole hangin' out under the shed.   I don't care a cent
When I hear them frogs, who pays the rent.

Me an' Mandy set on the porch a talkin'
But when them peterdicks go to squawkin'
I just stop.   Seems I get so drowsy just along
About the middle of their sing song.

I sometimes most wish I was a frog and contented,
Whether I owned a big farm or rented
Somebody else's.   Then a feller wouldn't need to worry,
Whether the plowin was done and  never have to hurry.

So 'long in the spring of the year
There haint nothin' I like to hear,
Nor nothin' I am half so fond
Of listen' to as them frogs down in that pond.

# The Spring Equinox.

All day the elements have had
  A fierce, malignant war.
Across the budding fields of spring
  Aeolus drives his car.

'Tis winter's last and weakest fight,
  For a few days will bring,
Ah, we will hail it with delight,
  The young and sprightly spring.

Then blow winter while you may.
  Your scattered snow flakes round,
For spring quite soon will be this way,
  And you no longer found.

## Good Night.

The sun sinks down behind the hills,
  Good night.
The bird its last sweet carol trills,
  Good night.
The sun is gone,
The birds' song stilled.
All sounds are hushed
And silence reigns
  Good night.

The moon upon us sheds her light
  Good night.
Across our love hath come a blight,
  Good night.
Love's flame is out:
'Twill burn no more.
You blew it out
Thus let it stay,
  Good night.

# A Recollection.

(BY AN OLD BACHELOR.)

What do I remember of that childish face? Ah, 'tis one of those sad sweet spots in the fields of memory to which I will ever turn though each visit makes my heart swell and a tear steal down a furrow in my cheek.

But my pipe is out. Here is a match from the deepest corner of my vest pocket. Now the wreaths of smoke curl upward and I see that childish face once more. It is—yes it is— the face of Alice, my child sweet-heart. Who does not remember the loves of childhood? Those sweet childish experiences when we, fresh from the bosom of God, do not know that love is something to be hidden. When we would take each other's tiny hands and stand looking into one another's faces well knowing that there was something pulling our hearts together but caring not what it was.

Alice was the good angel of my childhood's years. Her father's house was just at the edge of our farm—for I am country born and often here in the smoke and din of the city I wish that I could again see the green meadows and play at hide and seek in the old barn. Quite often would tiny Alice come toddling over to our house to play with me, the morning dew kissing her little pink feet into blushes as she waded through the wet still grass, and for her lips I always had a kiss. She was five and I was six. What days of joy were these when we, hand in hand, went to search where that loudly cackling hen had made her nest, or it may be we went to wade in the brook and catch the frightened polliwogs in our hands.

Each was anxious to share the sorrows and joys of the other. I remember how she cried in sympathy with me one day when I cut my finger with my brother's big knife I had taken without his leave from his Sunday trousers pocket.

Then, too, when her pet robin died I was chief mourner as we took its tiny dead body out under an apple tree and made for it a suitable grave. I realy think the sermon I preached as she patted the soft earth over it was a model, at least for tenderness and sympathy that might well be used by many today when hearts are bowed in sadnesss.

No sweetmeat was ever eaten by one unless the other shared and I remember when one day she had a big blushing cherry in her fingers, and I would not take a taste of it she was about to cry. "Cause," said she, "if you don't eat some it won't taste good."

One day when I was at her home as we came in from play Alice ran hastily to her mother saying: "Mamma I want you to teach me to cook and keep house."

"Why, what for, dear," said her mother.

"'Cause me and Chic (my real name was Will) are going to get married before long and I want to know how to keep my house nice like you do yours," said Alice confidentially.

Her mother assured her that she would teach her in due time, and we again hastened out to play with well contented hearts.

Blessings on child lovers. Purity in their minds, carelessness in their hearts and love in every action.

And now my recollection brings me to our first winter at school. Alice's home was immediately on the path that led across the field to the little rugged school house a quarter of a mile away. I was an only child, with no brother or sister to accompany me to school, but I never lacked company. As I came whistling across the field toward Alice's home I always saw a child's face pressed against the window pane, more rosy and sweet, I thought, than the geraniums that nodded on the sill beneath it. When I reached the house she was always standing on the door step, her chubby little hands ensconced in red mittens of her mother's making, a warm hood of the same color on her head and in her hand a little tin pail which held her noon lunch. Beneath her arm was her primer, but this I was always too gallant to let her carry.

Away we scampered to the school house, stopping perchance to watch a squirrel as he frisked to and fro on the now barren branches of his oak tree home, then hastening on lest we be late and receive a frown from our teacher, who was one of those old fashioned followers of the rod who would have thought it beneath his dignity to smile. Those were withal happy days at school though to me the noon hour was the most pleasant when Alice and I left the other children and built our play houses by ourselves like the two selfish midgets that we were.

We did not always escape punishment, and more than once, I especially, had to endure some such terrible ordeal as standing on the floor on one foot, or sitting on the dunce block. There was one punishment, though, that even now I remember with great pleasure and a tinge of sadness.

It was a rule that for paltry offenses the boys should sit with the girls. Alice was my seat mate and the punishment was not severe.

Thus the school term swept by until the last month had come and neither I nor Alice had missed a day. With pleasure we looked forward to the last day of school, when our teacher had promised to relax his severity and give us a treat in the way of a holiday. Just twenty school days remained, when on a Monday morning pshaw! there is a lump in my throat—as I drew near the home of my child sweetheart, I failed to see her face.

"Alice is sick. She has a very sore throat," said her mother, in answer to my inquiring look as I opened the door.

I trudged on to school, but if the squirrels frisked I did not see them and if any bird sang I failed to hear. All I recollect is that I felt very chilly and sad. Neither Tuesday nor the three following days brought any smiling face to the window. On Friday her mother called to me as I passed and requested that I tell my mother to come over that night, as Alice was much worse. After supper my father, mother and I all went to her home. Alice's mother and my own held an anxious conversation with the family doctor very soon after we arrived, and while I heard but little of it one word, "diphtheria," sticks in my memory like a poisoned arrow.

After a while we all went into the room where Alice was. When I saw her pale face, once so rosy, and her sunken eyes my childish heart was struck with terror. I had not seen her during her sickness. I know why now, but then I thought it wonderfully cruel. Indeed it was only with constant begging that I got my mother's consent on that sad night. A faint smile spread over her face as she saw me, and she tried to speak but it was only a whisper. I bent over her to kiss her parched lips, but they drew me away, and I burst into tears. For hours, it seemed an age to me, we sat by her bed and no one spoke. Every few minutes the doctor would go to her and every time turned away with a more troubled look. At last he whispered something to her father and both of them went and stood by her bed.

She had lain quiet for a long time, but now she turned uneasily and seemed to be struggling. All gathered round her bed and as she tossed to and fro struggling for her breath, her little face bore such a look of suffering that all burst into tears.

Then she was easy for a moment. "She is dying," said the doctor.

"Papa," she whispered, "where do people go when they die?"

It seemed that his big manly heart would burst as he realized that soon his idol was to be torn from him and he replied: "You will go to heaven, my dear."

The little sufferer looked around the tearful group, and as her eyes rested upon me she smiled and a strange light came into her eyes as she said: "May Chic go with me?"

Ah, Alice, as you look down from that realm of spirits

where you now are crowned with lilies white as your pure soul, do you ever wish that my poor battered spirit was your companion? Heartily did I wish that I could be your companion on that night. It was with that smile on her face that she closed her eyes. Patient, loving, faithful Alice, my child sweetheart, was dead.

That is my first recollection, but why are my cheeks so wet and why am I choking so—over only a recollection.

## Poem.

READ BEFORE THE ALUMNI OF THE FAIRMONT NORMAL SCHOOL
AT FAIRMONT, WEST VIRGINIA, JUNE 8, 1898.

As a friendly touch of a friendly hand
Is warm to the pulse in a foreign land,

As a cooling draught to lips that are dry,
Neath the noonday sun in a copper sky,

As an oasis green in a desert vast,
Is the remembrance sweet of days that are past.

So the chapel steps I mount once more,
And stand entranced at the chapel door.

I look within; before my eyes
An oft familiar scene doth rise.
Two hundred student girls and boys,
Just in the heyday of their joys,
With whispers sly and flying notes
That sail like tiny fairy boats,
Across the intervening space,
Until they meet a blushing face.
Each note is tucked within a book
And read with many a watchful look,
Lest teachers catch them unawares
And five demerits then be theirs.
Then from the Book which all endures,
Somewhat is read that peace insures.
All heads are bowed, all heads are bared,
All pray, or study lessons unprepared.
When this is o'er the jingling bell
A well known sound makes, 'tis the knell
Of this brief respite, hour of pleasure,
Fun and mischief without measure.
Begrudge us not those happy days,
They now have flown like flitting jays,
And all we have that aye shall last,
The sweet remembrance of the past.

i meet you tonight and I greet you,
  Friends of the days gone by;
We have toiled in the storm and the tempest,
  We have laughed neath a smiling sky.

We have laughed, we have wept, I tell you,
  We have fought the battle of life,
Now some are laurel crowned victors,
  There are some who fell in the strife.

The race to the swift not always,
  Nor conquerors always the strong.
But honor to him who fights bravely,
  Though the battle may not be long.

A tear for those who have fallen,
  A smile for those who have won;
And a shout for all who fought bravely
  Until the battle was done.

A million wheeling worlds in space,
  Ten thousand blazing suns.
Controlled are governed held in place
  By might of mind alone.

There's terror in the earthquake's shock,
  A horror in the howling wind,
More terrible and mightier far
  Are daring feats of mind.

Unto his triumphal car this God
Doth bind all other powers
And moving forces,   The lightning
Is his willing and obedient slave,
And with winged feet doth haste
To execute the slightest wish of mind.
The roaring winds swell sails
That haste to friendly ports
Rich merchantmen.   The dire destroying
Fire that brave Prometheus stole
Warms the temple in which mind dwells,
How soon we know not this haughty God,
This mind, shall bid the winds to blow or cease.
The rain to fall or drouth to starve the plain.

The earth to tremble or be still.
How soon shall he the troubled wave
Becalm or placid waters heave on high,
Perchance ere long this God, this mind
Shall haughty grow and bid the
Spinning worlds to stop and blazing suns
To cease to shine,
Who knows, can think, or yet predict
How great a God this mind may yet become.

The mind is mighty but I greet
The thought of friendship as more sweet
And lasting than the mind's great feat
    That makes up wonder.

A kindly heart it seems to me
Is more than sweetest minstrelsy
Or glorious deed of chivalry,
    E'en though it blunder.

I love the friendly warm hand clasp,
The sure and heartfelt friendship grasp.
'Twill be remembered when a gasp
    Parts us forever.

I think it is but little worth
If names are famous o'er the earth
And in the heart there is a dearth
    Of kindly greetings.

When Gœthe's mighty soul
Had reached the goal
And he was passing into night
He cried " More light!"

Let this be your cry, brother,
More light for one another;
More light to know the pain
That follows greedy gain.

There are cries in the street
And the faces we meet
Are pinched by want and need,
There's sorrow and care
That we may share
If the cries of our brothers we heed.

More strength, more light,
More courage to fight,
That evil things may die.
More strength more light
That the darkness of night
Be changed to a smiling day.

Though I can never sing Homeric songs
Or untold wealth of Croesus claim,
I hope I shall be known to fame,
As one who did a friend no wrong.

There's little virtue, little worth
If warm blood flows not in the heart.
In riches, station, beauty, art,
There's yet a mighty dearth.

When riches wing themselves away,
When fortunes crumble into dust,
'Tis then you need a friend to trust,
To trust and cling to in that day.

# The Island of Despair.

It was called the "Island of Despair." But why it should have had such a name I can but let you imagine. The island itself had the appearance of a pleasure garden, at least to one who had never lived upon it. Warm breezes came over the sea and pressed their languid lips to the ever blooming flowers. Birds with beautiful plumage and, what is remarkable, with sweet songs in their throats, flew from branch to branch, or hopped among the tall grass and brilliant flowers. When the morning sun arose ten million million diamond drops of dew glistened in the light. At night the moon saw its soft reflection in clear streams that looked like silver bands binding the island to the ocean. The dwellers on this fair spot were not incapable of enjoyment. There were no aged persons there. No one was ever born; no one ever died. Beautiful women, sisters of Venus they must have been, arrayed in the most costly garments, bedecked with priceless jewels, were the only representatives of their sex to be found on the island. Yet it was called the "Island of Despair." Men, young men, with strength in their sinews and red blood in their veins were the constant companions of the beautiful women. For all this it was called, this island, "The Island of Despair."

No one was ever happy on the island. Continual misery and dissatisfaction gnawed at the hearts of those who lived upon it. "Why is this beautiful island called the Island of Despair?" I asked of the stalwart, handsome young man, who had picked up me, a shipwrecked traveler, in his pleasure boat and taken me to his home. "Ah! you have not yet learned the secret of our misery," said he. "I will tell you. This is called the 'Island of Despair,' because we who live upon it know nothing of what romancers and poets call Love. We have no part in the trinity of father, mother, child. We are not included in the cycle birth, life, death. We call love a fanciful conjuration of a diseased brain. Selfishness is the rule of our lives"

It was thus the young man spoke, the young man who had spent a million years of youth on the beautiful island where selfishness was the rule of life and where Love was not known. Then I thought of the name of the island and I understood why it was called the "Island of Despair."

## Reciprocity.

(BY A BACK COUNTRY PHILOSOPHER.)

You have seen the mighty tyrant
A swayin' of the throne,
An' oppressin' of his subjects
And never hear 'em moan.
You have called him hard and cruel,
Thought all feelin' he did lack;
But never mind about him for
He will get it all back.

You have seen a cruel father,
When hardened he had grown,
And his children begged for bread,
A givin' of a stone.
And when they asked for mercy
They would get another whack,
But you can rest assured
He will get it all back.

Sometimes we send our money
Away to heathen lands,
And use our precious savin's
To convert the savage bands.
And they think we're spendin' money
To show 'em the right track,
But unless they're mighty slick
We will get it all back.

The merchant aint jist honest;
Mixes sugar and some sand.
The seemin' upright farmer
Plays a half dishonest hand.
And they think no one will know it
If they are a little slack,
But don't you be afraid,
They will get it all back.

## RECIPROCITY.

So I could keep a singin'
An' a tellin' in my song,
Of the lots and lots of people
That do somethin' that is wrong.
And they think it makes no difference
If no one is on the track,
But you may be quite certain
They will get it all back.

## The Poet.

Some are wont to make light of poets.    Who has not smiled sometime in his life at the puerile effusions of some versifier? By him who is not guilty shall the first stone be cast.    The musty and moss-covered jokes about the spring poet, his long hair, his shiny clothes, et cetera, are too current for comment. Shall we laugh at the poet, the versifier or the mere scribbler of lines?    Not so.    To me there is no verse that does not seem like a voice from a better land.    I usually read the poetry in our magazines first of all.    And where, pray you, may worse poetry be found than between the covers of our most highly respectable magazines.    Not in this book, I pray.

But it is not for beautiful thoughts and polished expression alone one reads poetry.    There is a rhythm in nature.    There is a music of the spheres.    "Such harmony is in immortal souls" and every poem, every verse, however feeble and weak, is a beat of that rhythm, a note of that music, a chord of that harmony.

Poetry is the youth of the soul; prose is its manhood.    All literatures attest that poetry is the earlier form.    After the mind is developed it reasons, and reasoning is death to the imagination.    Who can even imagine that Shakespeare would have towered to such heights of thought or so carefully unwound the tangle of human passions had he been more highly educated.

So hither all ye warblers of springtime ballads, in me you will find a friend and defender.    Your rhymes may be false, your accents awry, and your feet maimed and halt, but your hearts are pure, and for that I love you.

## Requital.

Ah well-a-day! we sow and reap not;
We toil, grow thin and pale:
We rack our brains and sleep not,
That those who follow after
May fill their lives with laughter,
Have rich harvests and be hale.

## A Translation.

Among my literary curiosities I have the following letter written by a young man, very poor, to a very rich and beautiful lady, with whom he was at one time in love, but having been spurned, came to hate her. As the original is in Persian, I take the liberty to translate it:

"Most Fair Queen: Once I loved you, now I loathe you. Once you were the idol of my eye, the inspiration of my muse; now you are hateful to my sight. How you strut in your finery! But I tell you the time will come when all your silks will be moth-eaten, all your finery will be dust. That sparkling diamond on your finger will at last clasp only a bone. Your eyes that so sparkle now will sometime fall through their sockets and waste away in your hollow skull. Those breasts white as snow and polished as ivory shall be eaten of worms. Those arms that once could have transported me to heaven by a single embrace will then be a terror to behold. Thy throat from which now such sweet music comes will be the highway of the devouring worm. Living, moving, singing, I hate thee; dead, festering, rotting, I abhor thee. All in all, I despise, I detest, I scorn, I curse, I hate you.

Your one time lover, but now your evil genius.

OMAR HAH-KANEM.

# Medley.

POEM READ BEFORE THE WEST VIRGINIA EDITORIAL ASSOCIATION AT WESTON, WEST VIRGINIA, MAY 21ST, 1897.

I've got up here to read my piece,
  Before this august body,
And should I own the honest truth
  I'm feelin' rather "shoddy!"

If I could write like Shakespeare,
  Or even like Longfellow,
I'd get up here and read a poem
  And wouldn't feel so mellow.

But that I can't as you well know,
  At least I think you ought to,
But I am billed to read a piece,
  And this is what I have brought you.

The office goat is hungry,
  And if you don't like what I read,
I've yet this consolation—
  The goat can have a feed.

First I pray you listen
  Unto a little ditty.
In haste 'tis writ—don't publish it—
  About this little City.

## ODE TO WESTON.

Hail thou Weston! Pleasant City,
  Sitting 'mong the verdant hills,
With a carpet spread before you,
  Watered by the silver rills.
There is rest beneath your shade trees,
  There is peace within your homes,
Which your wandering son remembers,
  Little matter where he roams.

Fair the skies that bend above you,
  Fair the stars that glitter down;
But no fairer than thy daughters
  Dwelling in their native town.

Pure the waters rippling round you
　　That from mountain fountains came.
But the virtues of thy daughters
　　Make the waters blush for shame.

Strong the hills that rise around you
　　Beckoning us to higher ken,
But the strength of all your hill-tops
　　Matches not your mighty men.
And methinks were you destroyed,
　　Leveled by the licking fire,
All thy sons would straight betake them
　　Build thee!  Build thee ever higher.

Long, ah long shall I remember
　　How we fared in Weston town
In the guest room of our memories
　　All your gifts are noted down.
When again our eyes shall see thee
　　It is truly hard to tell,
But our hearts will say in parting,
　　"Beauteous Weston, Fare-the-well!"

———o———

The next thing that I bring you
　　Is the Editors' little song,
Which has at least one merit,
　　It isn't very long.

He sits in his office weary-
　　The ink he cannot sling.
He feels so awful bummy,
　　And thus begins to sing.

### EDITOR'S SONG.

Life is dreary,
I am weary,
　　And the copy hook is bare;
I was out last night
And cannot write,
　　So I swear and pull my hair.

Hope is fled—
I wish I were dead.

And through the gates on high.
The pressman Joe
Has stumped his toe,
  An two galleys are now in pi.

The "devil" is sick,
The ink is thick,
  And the pony refuses to go.
I think I'll sell
And move to—well
  Where little birds don't shovel snow.

A list of arrears,
Covering several years,
  With no hopes they will ever pay:
Still I hoe my row,
But I've got no dough—
  Oh, I am a miserable jay!

——o——

But while he is singing so happy and gay,
An irate subscriber is passing that way,
And dropped in the office with horse-whip and gun,
And the editor passed through the back door on a run.

Then down in his bed room he sits him and thinks
Of the hardness of life and the softness of drinks—
And while he is following along in this strain,
These are the thoughts that flit through his brain.

### A RETROSPECT.

When Paris to his Trojan home
  Led back his Grecian bride,
And bore her safely in his bark
  Across the raging tide.
Then Menelaus, the one bereft,
  Cut up some ugly capers,
But not a one the story read
  In the next morning's papers.

When Caesar led his Roman-hosts
  Away up in old Gaul,

He met the bearded Gothic men
  And drove them to the wall.
The noble Romans left behind
  Could do naught else but choose
To wait some months for tidings—
  There was no *Daily News.*

Then when old Alexander
  Had conquered all the world
And all his troops were sent away
  And all his banners furled,
He could not sit him down at night
  After affairs diurnal,
And see his name and read his fame
  Writ in the *Daily Journal.*

When down to Egypt Caesar went
  And carried war's allarums,
Subduing Cleopatra fair,
  By daring deeds of arms.
The leathery gossip at his home
  With envy turned not green,
For no Egyptian special
  Brought tidings of the scene.

— —o— —

And now, good friends. I pray you,
  Come listen unto me,
And I will close my doggerel
  With an apostrophe.

AN APOSTROPHE.

Well now, my friends, ye editors,
  Ye wielders of the pen,
Who educate the populace
  And mold the minds of men,
From every town and hamlet,
  From every pleasant hill,
From where the beech and chestnut
  Hang o'er the rippling rill.

From where the broad Potomac
  Slips silent to the sea,

# MEDLEY.

To where the rough Kanawha
  Rolls onward to the lea.
And from the smiling meadows
  That line Ohio's shore,
To where Monongahela's tides
  Flow on forever more.

From every plain and wooded height
  You have gathered here today,
Like knights prepared for battle,
  And ready for the fray.
To gather inspiration
  And to clasp each other's hands,
To bind your hearts together
  As though with iron bands.

To increase hope and courage
  To help you on your way;
To touch the lute of friendship,
  That it may happy play—
You have come from every section
  To Weston town today.

And let me say in closing,
  When homeward you shall turn,
Let on the altars of your hearts
  The fires of friendship burn;
So when again you grasp your pen,
  I pray you wield it well—
And now, my brother editors,
  I bid you all farewell!

## Confreres.

In the pages that follow will be found verses taken at random from the writings of some of my friends. These are not intended as representative of their best work, but are such as I had at hand. They are inserted here, not with the knowledge and consent of the writers, but on my own responsibility, because I think them worth preserving.

H. L. SWISHER.

## Success.

Two ships sail over the harbor bar
  With the flush of the morning breeze,
And both are bound for a haven far
  O'er the shimmering summer seas.

With sails all set, fair wind and tide,
  They steer for the open main;
But little they reck of the billows wide
  E'er they anchor safe again.

There is one, perchance, e'er the summer is done,
  That reaches the port afar,
She hears the sound of the welcoming gun
  As she crosses the harbor bar.

The haven she reaches, success, 'tis said
  Is the end of a perilous trip,
Perchance e'en the bravest and best are dead
  Who sailed in the fortunate ship.

The other bereft of shroud and sail,
  At the mercy of wind and tide,
Is swept by the might of the pitiless gale
  'Neath the billows dark and wide.

But 'tis only the one in the harbor there
  That receiveth the meed of praise;
The other sailed when the morn was fair
  And was lost in the stormy ways.

And so to the men who have won renown
  In the weary battle of life,
There cometh at last the victor's crown;
  Not to him who fell in the strife.

For the world recks not of those who fail,
  Nor cares what their trials are.
Only praises the ship that with swelling sail
  Comes in o'er the harbor bar.
                          —M. S. Cornwell,

## When Dad Strikes Ile.

If dad strikes ile—oh, how it makes me smile!
  He says he'll fit me out in fine things,
An' I always will be dressed, jes' in the very best,
  An' I'll wear a heap o' rings—
    When dad strikes ile.

If dad strikes ile, I'll neither bake ner' bile;
  I'll hev all the house work done;
An' the organ I will play all through the blessed day,
  An' I'll jes' hev lots of fun
    When dad strikes ile.

If dad strikes ile, all the girls I'll quickly rile;
  Their eyes I'll turn a grassy green,
Fer I'll use up every art to break the manly heart,
  An' I'll be the village queen
    When dad strikes ile.

If dad strikes ile, I'll drive the easy mile
  To the preachin' every Sunday afternoon,
In a buggy bright and new—an' I'll hev company too—
  Oh, I hope it will be soon,
    When dad strikes ile!

                —*John Wallace.*

## The Mariner's Love.

"The continuous roar
Of the surf on the shore,
As it dashes its wild billows high,
Makes sweet music to me,
Born and bred by the sea,
Where the sea gull and storm petrels fly.

And if ever should I,
From the sea forced to fly,
Settle down in some far distant land;
Where the surf billow's roar
Came to me never more,
Or salt breeze my brow gently fanned;
Then I hope that e'er long
(Though the hope may be wrong),
That the God to whom we seamen pray,
Will look down from the sky
And permit me to die,"
Said a mariner bold from the bay.

Years had passed since the time
When the man in his prime
Had spoken these brave words to me;
And that mariner bold
Had grown gray and old,
And had left his old home by the sea.
For when storm witches rave
O'er the foam covered wave,
Naught but strength can their fury withstand;
And when muscle and brawn
Are with fleeting years gone
An old man is far better on land.

In a far inland town,
O'er which grim mountains frown,
On his death-bed our mariner lay;
Each laboring sigh
And his slow glazing eye
Told his life sands were ebbing away.
Spoke the mariner low:

" My lads, will you go
And carry me back to the sea,
And dig me a grave
Where the incoming wave
Will heap the salt sea-weed o'er me?"

And now there's a mound,
Where the murmuring sound
Of the breakers that play on the shore,
Make sweet music to him
Who was once wont to stem
E'en their wildest weird warring of yore.

  *  *  *  *  *

Years have passed since that time;
I have long passed my prime;
And I stand old and as feeble as he,
Before me the grave,
And beyond it the wave
That its occupant once loved to see.

What's the moral?   Well, you,
Who have loved and are true,
Will scarce ask the moral of me.
Here a hero lies dead,
And over his head
Croons the voice of his life's love, the sea.

       *Geo. M. Ford.*

## The Dead Sure Thing.

My son, in all your progress
Through this sinful vale of tears,
In all your plans and projects
In all the coming years,
Upon this bit of wisdom
Let your mind all changes ring,
The most elusive thing in nature.
    Is
       the
          dead
              sure
                  thing.

You may toil and you may struggle
In a bitter fight with fate,
But you'd better true accept it
Before it is too late,
It's as certain as that time endures
And its truth all ages sing,
The most elusive thing in nature
    Is
       the
          dead
              sure
                  thing.

The most bitter pill to swallow,
The sharpest pang of all,
Comes when pride of certain victory
Has gone before the fall;
But the final, firm acceptance

Of this truth removes the sting,
The most elusive thing in nature
         Is
             the
                 dead
                         sure
                                 thing.


Then defeat is but a milestone
On the road to victory.
Each rebuff will only help you
Your mistake each time to see,
If to this word of warning
You will let your spirit cling,
The most elusive thing in nature
         Is
             the
                 dead
                         sure
                                 thing.

                        —*Justin M. Kunkle.*

## On Tumble-Down Street.

On Tumble-Down Street's the boss place to have fun,
'Cause there you can play at Black-man and run
Ever'where, an' do jes anything 'at you like—
There's where Dick Martin lives, an's big brother Ike.

Gee-mo-me! I'd ruther be Dick, pore's he is,
'An to be President. I would, 'y gee whizz!
Ef I could only live on Tumble-Down Street,
Even ef you don't get good things to eat.

What's cookies and pies when you jes got plenty!
One's better when you've hooked it an' *twenty*
'At your mother gives you to run out and play—
Druther have the one 'at you hook'd, any day.

On Tumble-Down Street on'y pore people lives,
But I wish't to goodness we lived there, fer't gives
Me the lonesomes up here where things is so fine
'At you can't live at your ease  -I'm jes a dyin'

To live way down there on old Tumble-Down Street;
Wear raggedy clo'se an' go in my bare feet —
W'y, there you don't have to wash more'n once a week,
Ner dress up on Sunday and look so blame meek—

Jes like you didn't want to go fishin', you know,
Ner wouldn't think, even, of goin' a swimmin', tho'
You're all the time longin', plannin' an' wishin'
'At you could run away an' go swimmin' er fishin'.

Tell you what! Tumble-Down Street's the place to live!
Dog my cats, ef that aint right! An' I wouldn't give
A day on Tumble-Down Street fer a life-time
Where we live, an' ever'thing's so dog-gone fine.

I was goin' to tell you—purt nigh forgot!
'At Dick Martin's little sister, they call "Dot,"
'S the purtiest girl ever saw in my life!
An' some day, mebbe, Dick's sister'll be my wife!
—C. Luke Michael.

## Yesterday.

O yesterday, oh yesterday!
Oh day that is forever spent,
What was your purpose or intent?
Why were you on your errand sent,
To speed so rapidly away?

You came with morning's brightest ray,
And quickly after you arrived,
By skill and effort you contrived    ·
To have all nature's work revived,
And bring her forces into play.

You left us as the moon's pale beam
Was casting down its fainter hue,
Just as the stars came into view.
And o'er the earth the darkness grew
From hill-top to the winding stream.

Came you to see what was achieved
By man in search for something new?
Or what he may have learned to do,
That none before him ever knew?
If so, you saw much and believed.

Or. did you come with sword in hand,
That man on man might war declare?
That many hearts should know despair,
While even wives and daughters fair
Fall victims to the savage band?

Or maybe you came in robes of white,
That men might learn to be at peace,
The starving prisoners to release,
From cruel wars and strifes to cease
And turn their hearts to what is right.

Yes, all of this you've done and seen,
Yov've passed the desert brown and bare,
The woodland with it's flowers rare,
You've breathed the purest mountain air,
And smiled upon the meadows green.

Some broken hearts you left to moan,
To sigh and shed the bitter tear
At loss of some one, loved and dear,
Who has gone from pain and fear,
And griefs that never will be known.

But others you found as glad and gay
As is the bird upon the tree;
While some were toiling like the bee,
Some were oppressed, and others free,
Such changing scenes viewed in a day.

How various are the tasks you've done;
Some anxious heart you taught to pray,
Some youth from duty led astray,
And gray heads you have made more gray,
From morn to setting of the sun.

You've lifted some from poverty,
Some fortunes gained, while others lost,
Some on financial waves were tossed,
And like a ship the storm had crossed,
When riding on an angry sea.

Now tell us from the unseen past
Where you have made your habitation.
Tell why so short was your duration,
And gone as with a conflagration,
While shadows dim the lamp light cast.
                                    —*Jas. W. Horn.*

## The Isle of Going-to-be.

Far out yonder on the misty sea,
Fringed with bright flowers eternally,
Lies the fair Isle of Going-to-be.

And birds are warbling sweet melody,
The lilies nod and beckon me
Out to this Isle of Going-to-be.

Sail out with the tide in merry glee!
Sail out in youth while 'tis plain to see
This magic Isle of Going-to-be!

For waves of doubt foam 'round o'er the lea,
And we ne'er reach this isle in the sea—
This phantom Isle of Going-to-be.

*C. Luke Michael.*

## The Little White Kerchief and Pennies of Gold.

*The white kerchief and pennies of gold!*
Oh, what a love story all these could unfold!
No gold ever sparkled as bright as her eyes,
And they were as blue as the depth of the skies.

I gave them in token of love never told—
*The little white kerchief and pennies of gold.*
Oh, could she but know of the love she has lost,
The tears and the heartaches this lost love has cost!

No flower ever bloomed whose tints were so rare
As the blush on her cheeks—no sunshine so fair.
*The little white kerchief and pennies of gold—*
I would they were mine—mine ever to hold!

But my heart has grown weary waiting so long,
And my soul never hums but a desolate song.
The fires of my love have gone out and grown cold
*O'er the little white kerchief and pennies of gold.*

*C. Luke Michael.*

## I'm Goin' Home fer Christmas.

I'm goin' home fer Christmas—back to the old homestead!
Fer dad's writ me quite a letter and says that Jim and Ned,
And Billy, my scapegoat brother, and Jane, 'long with her man,
In fact, we'll all be there; the hull caboose and van!
And even Uncle 'Lige's days o' fussin' were all past.
Thet the quarrel 'bout their hoss trade was sure to be the last,
And thet mother wuz feelin' poorly, but he reckoned she'd be
   spry
If she had us all to cook fer as in the days gone by.

So I'm goin' home fer Christmas, and I wonder when I go
If I'll gas around like others thet our country ways air slow.
I know thet Abner Burton, jest home from a city school,
And one o' the Smiths, who'd travelled some, us' to ridicule
The style o' clothes we allus wore; and the way we carried on
They said would shock a feller who'd seen the gay bon ton.
And they axed old Hiram Peters how he passed the time away:
Said Hiram, ruther dry like—"A-passin' the time o' day."

But when the train pulls in and dad's a-standin' there
And waitin' with the family rig and my old fav'rite mare,
As he grabs my hands so warmly thet I'm skeered I'll lose an
   arm,
I'll holler out the praises o' the greetin's o' the farm.
And when he's sized me up and told me how I've growed
I'll busy him with questions as we drive along the road;
I'll ax him 'bout the neighbors, and who be married off—
But 'bout the squire's darter, I'll kind o' hem and cough.

Yes, I'm goin' home fer Christmas, and already I kin see
The old home by the willers jest as it us' to be;
The night drops down her shadders, but ev'ry winder pane
Gleams out its streaks o' gladness in a welcome home again;
And the house dog barks mycom in', as we drive in through
   the gate,
To the failin' ears o' mother; and she fidgets 'bout the wait,
Till my kisses chase the wrinkles from off the haunts o' care—
Oh, I'm gittin too impatient, but on Christmas I'll be there!

                                        *John Wallace.*

## Expectation.

On the shore of the ocean of life I am sitting
  And looking far out on its watery waste,
Where the sea seems to meet the fleecy clouds, flitting
  'Thwart the sky where the line of horizon is traced.

In patience and hope many years I have waited
  For the ship of my dreams to rise o'er the crest,
And bring me the treasures with which it is freighted,
  The realization of hope unconfessed.

But the ship of my visions is not yet in sight,
  And hope once so strong, is beginning to die.
Yet still I sit waiting from morning till night
  Every day, and still hope that my ship will draw nigh.

                *J. Cal. Watkins.*

## A Sylvan Tragedy.

Like sentinels sear, the oak trees stand,
  As they stood ages agone;
Guarding the gates to a wonderland
  Where the beautiful sleep on.

Where the beautiful sleep, and may hope to dream
  Of a world that can not wake,
For the world lies beyond the gurgling stream
  And beyond the edging lake.

The sear leaves fall, and the green leaves shoot
  From the buds and mosses twine,
O'er the fallen trunks their leaves minute,
  Their leaves the hue of the pine.

By the sentinels tall, comes the forests' foe
  And starts the hare to its den,
He whistles a warning now high, now low,
  Which echoes, then dies again.

He muddies the stream in its shallow bed
  As he crosses but does not slack,
When the loose soil presses beneath his tread
  And the flowers lie bruised in his track.

"I will strike at the heart," doubtless thinks the foe,
  For at a giant's root he stops,
He severs its bark at a single blow
  And deepens the wound as he chops.

At his stroke the birds in the lowest round
  Of its branches start and cry,
The nestlings answer with feeble sound
  And flutter helplessly.

Another, another, the blows fall fast,
  Till the boughs begin to sway.
Exultingly strikes he the mighty last,
  And its very heart gives way.

The crash is a knell to the lesser growth.
  A dirge for the nestlings, too,
The oak and the birds have fallen, both,
  By the hand of the forests' foe.

But a monument stands where the deed was done,
  And o'er it the green bough bends;
'Tis the woodman's home, built of mighty oaks,
  And the birds are his dearest friends.

*Alice Piersol-Cain.*

www.ingramcontent.com/pod-product-compliance
Lightning Source LLC
Chambersburg PA
CBHW032146010726
47493CB00008BA/2595